# The Iberian Guard

*Shadows of the Reformation*

By Tommy Russo

**Chapter 1: The Summons**

Dawn crept into the silent halls of the Vatican, casting golden rays across the marble floors and illuminating the intricate artwork on the towering walls. The early morning quiet was broken only by the steady footsteps of Santiago de León, Captain of the Iberian Guard, as he moved through a dimly lit corridor. Each step echoed with centuries of devotion, duty, and sacrifice.

In his hand, Santiago held a letter marked with the Pope's seal—a simple design bearing a heavy meaning. Summoned at dawn by Pope Leo X himself, Santiago knew this was no ordinary meeting. The weight of the papal seal and the urgency of the summons told him a grave mission awaited.

Santiago approached the door to the Pope's private study, his heart steady yet heavy. He knew every turn of the Vatican's labyrinthine halls by heart; they were his second home, a place that protected him even as it held him captive to his vows. As he paused at the ornate door, he touched the symbol of his order on the ring he wore—a reminder of his vow to serve. He whispered a brief prayer before entering.

A servant opened the door, bowing respectfully. The study was lined with books, manuscripts, and scrolls, all bearing the weight of centuries of theological thought. Behind a grand desk sat Pope Leo X, a man in his late fifties with features etched by both authority and weariness. Despite his age, his gaze was sharp and unwavering.

"Captain Santiago," Pope Leo's voice, though soft, resonated with authority. The room fell still, and Santiago stepped forward, bowing on one knee.

"Your Holiness, I am at your service."

The Pope motioned for Santiago to rise. "Rise, my son. We have matters of great importance to discuss."

As Santiago stood, he felt the weight of the Pope's gaze upon him. Though Pope Leo was visibly aged, his eyes held a spark of determination—a reminder of the strength beneath the heavy mantle he bore.

"The Church faces a new kind of threat," the Pope began, his tone grave. "One that goes beyond heresy and calls into question the very fabric of our faith. You may have heard whispers of Martin Luther and his theses."

"Yes, Your Holiness. I have heard of him."

"Luther's ideas have spread like wildfire, igniting a dangerous curiosity among our flock. He claims to challenge corruption, but he endangers the souls of our people," Leo said, his voice filled with sorrow and anger. "This Reformation threatens to tear apart the unity of our Church."

The Pope gestured to a cardinal who stepped forward, presenting a parchment bearing a disturbing symbol: a coiled viper encircling a cross.

"This," Pope Leo continued, his voice sharp, "is the mark of a man who calls himself the Viper. He is no mere reformist. He is a zealot, an enemy who seeks to destroy the Church from within."

Santiago's brow furrowed as he studied the image. He had heard of the Viper only in whispered rumors—a shadowy figure leading a radical faction of Luther's followers. This Viper was no ordinary reformist; he was a manipulator, a man who exploited the fervor of reform to sow division and discord.

"The Viper leads a group called the Zealots of Veritas," Leo continued. "They are dangerous, hidden within the ranks of reformists, but their mission is darker still. They seek nothing less than the dismantling of our institution."

Pope Leo's voice softened, almost reverent. "They seek a text—the Codex Veritas—believed to contain knowledge that could destabilize our faith. If it exists, we must find it before they do."

The mention of the Codex stirred a mixture of dread and anticipation in Santiago's heart. The Codex Veritas was shrouded in myth, rumored to hold truths that could unravel the foundations of the Church itself.

Pope Leo's gaze locked onto Santiago's. "Captain, the task I set before you and the Guard is of utmost importance. You must locate and secure the Codex Veritas before it can be used to threaten the very soul of our Church."

Santiago bowed his head, his voice steady. "We will not fail, Your Holiness."

Pope Leo studied Santiago for a moment, the determination in his gaze softened by trust. "I know you will not. But be warned—the Viper's influence is pervasive. He has woven a network of loyalists within Luther's followers and among the common folk. Keep your faith close and your vigilance closer."

Santiago accepted the mission with a renewed determination. As he turned to leave, the Pope's voice stopped him one last time.

"Captain, a final word of caution."

Santiago looked back, attentive.

"Trust no one outside your Guard," Pope Leo said, his gaze piercing. "The Viper has allies in places we may not yet know. Guard your wisdom carefully."

Pope Leo watched Santiago closely, his gaze unyielding. He seemed to weigh every word before he spoke, as if he understood that the next few moments would shape the fate of the Church. The Pope gestured to the cardinal who stepped forward, holding another scroll. Unlike the others, this parchment was worn, its edges frayed with time, the ink faded but still legible.

"Captain Santiago," Leo began solemnly, "the Codex Veritas is not merely a book, nor is it a simple relic. It is something far more potent—a relic of such power that it could shape the faith of millions, either as a weapon or a testament. If it falls into the wrong hands, it could destroy not just our authority, but the foundation of belief that sustains our followers."

Santiago took in the Pope's words, feeling the weight of his responsibility deepen. He had known of relics that held symbolic power, artifacts cherished for their associations with saints and holy figures, revered by believers. But he sensed that the Codex Veritas was different—an object that seemed to embody both legend and fear, capable of changing the very narrative of the Church.

Pope Leo continued, his voice low. "The Codex Veritas is said to contain truths hidden from the public for centuries. Ancient knowledge, arcane texts, perhaps even writings from the time of Christ. But it is not these words alone that make it dangerous. Legends say it includes documents—historical records and interpretations—that could question our teachings or cast shadows on the pillars of faith we uphold."

The Pope's eyes, sharp and knowing, held Santiago's as he spoke. "Imagine what would happen if those who already doubt our authority found justification in these pages. Imagine the Zealots wielding this relic, spreading its knowledge to fuel their movement and undermine our foundations."

Santiago's jaw tightened. He knew that ideas could be as dangerous as swords. If the Codex contained even a fragment of what the Pope suggested, it was no wonder the Church had hidden it away, safeguarded from the hands of those who would misuse its power.

"The origins of the Codex are shrouded in mystery," Leo continued, turning his gaze toward the ancient relics that lined his study. "Some claim it was assembled by early scholars, scribes who saw the world in ways that transcended faith and tradition. Others say it holds fragments of pagan thought, philosophies considered too dangerous for the masses."

Santiago nodded, absorbing the implications. "Then this is not merely a mission to retrieve an artifact—it is a mission to protect the very soul of Christendom."

"Precisely," the Pope replied, his voice heavy. "The Codex Veritas, if misinterpreted, could become a tool for heresy, a weapon against the Church itself. And that is what the Viper seeks—a way to discredit us, to turn the minds of believers against us."

Santiago felt a deep chill settle over him, the gravity of his task looming larger than he had anticipated. His hand rested instinctively on the hilt of his sword, a silent reminder of the resolve that would guide him through the trials ahead.

"The Zealots of Veritas are relentless," Pope Leo continued, his voice unwavering. "They view faith as a shackle, binding humanity to ignorance. They believe that by revealing what lies within the Codex, they can liberate mankind from what they call the 'tyranny of belief.'"

The Pope shook his head, sadness mingling with resolve in his gaze. "But they do not understand faith, Captain. They see only words and doctrines, forgetting the countless lives that find purpose, hope, and salvation within those teachings."

He paused, his gaze softening as he looked at Santiago. "Our mission is not simply to defend a book, Santiago. It is to defend the lives, the souls, that depend on the truths we uphold."

Santiago met the Pope's gaze with unwavering resolve. "The Guard will secure the Codex, Your Holiness. We will not let it fall into the hands of those who seek to destroy us."

Pope Leo's face softened, a flicker of gratitude in his eyes. "Your faith and loyalty are a comfort in these dark times, my son. But be warned—the Codex will be defended fiercely. The Viper is cunning, and he knows our mission. He will not stop until he possesses it."

Leo gestured to the map that Santiago still held, tracing a finger over the regions where the Codex was rumored to be hidden. "Our sources believe it lies within a remote monastery in Germany, but the exact location is unknown. It is likely that only a handful of the oldest clerics within those walls know of its existence, let alone its hiding place."

Santiago examined the map closely, his mind already planning the journey. "We will reach Germany discreetly, posing as pilgrims or travelers if need be. The Guard is trained to be invisible."

"Good," Pope Leo said, nodding approvingly. "You must avoid drawing attention. Once the Zealots learn you are searching for the Codex, they will spare no effort to intercept you."

He glanced at the parchment one last time, his expression grim. "We live in times when ideas are more dangerous than swords, Santiago. When truth can be twisted into heresy with a single turn of phrase. The Viper knows this, and he will wield the Codex like a blade."

Santiago's gaze hardened. He had faced many enemies over the centuries, but none who sought to corrupt minds rather than control them. This mission was not merely about force—it was about understanding the danger of the ideas they were protecting, and the risks involved in allowing those ideas to reach a hostile world.

"Fear not, Your Holiness," Santiago said, his voice a steady vow. "We are prepared to fight, whether with words or with weapons."

The Pope's expression grew thoughtful. "Be mindful, Captain. Ideas cannot be slain with swords alone. Remember the words of Solomon: 'Wisdom is more precious than rubies, and all the things you may desire cannot compare with her.' You must guard your wisdom carefully."

Santiago nodded, feeling the ancient wisdom resonate within him. The Guard's faith was their greatest weapon, but it was also their shield. He understood that he would need both on this mission—to stay vigilant not only to physical threats but to the subtle danger of manipulation and doubt.

As he prepared to leave, Pope Leo took a step forward, placing a hand on Santiago's shoulder. "Go with God, Captain. And may He guide your steps, for they lead into darkness."

The weight of the Pope's blessing settled over him, a mantle of protection and duty. With a final bow, Santiago turned and exited the study, his steps echoing through the quiet halls. The Vatican felt like a fortress, an impregnable bastion of faith—but outside these walls, the forces that sought to tear it down were gathering strength.

As he returned to the Guard's quarters, he knew that the weight of his mission went beyond safeguarding a relic or silencing an enemy. It was about preserving the sanctity of faith itself, protecting the spirit that sustained the people he served.

With renewed resolve, Santiago made his way through the labyrinthine halls, feeling the centuries-old weight of his oath settle over him once more. This mission, he knew, would test every fiber of his being, every facet of his devotion. But he was ready, for he was a servant of the Church, bound by a vow that transcended time.

The weight of his conversation with Pope Leo lingered in Santiago's mind as he walked through the quiet corridors, heading back to the secluded chambers where the Iberian Guard made their home. These halls, ancient yet unchanged, were silent witnesses to countless moments of faith, loyalty, and sacrifice—qualities the Guard had embodied for centuries.

As he neared their quarters, Santiago felt a sense of solemnity settle over him, mingling with the duty he had carried since the day he had been anointed as one of the Guard. Each mission, each battle, each decade that passed had only deepened his understanding of what it meant to serve as a member of this order—a role that transcended the ordinary, rooted in a timeless oath and a bond unbreakable by age or decay.

The Guard's quarters lay beyond a hidden passage, tucked away from the prying eyes of the clergy and Vatican officials. Only a select few in the Church knew of their existence, and fewer still understood the extent of their devotion. Santiago entered the chamber, its walls lined with the armor, weapons, and artifacts the Guard had accumulated over centuries. Each item bore the weight of a thousand battles fought in the name of the Church, relics of a legacy that stretched beyond the scope of mortal lives.

Inside, his fellow Guards awaited him. Isabela, Marco, Emmanuel, and Rafael stood silently, their expressions solemn as they anticipated the task ahead. They, like Santiago, bore the unmarked years of devotion and sacrifice. They appeared to be in their prime—ageless, strong, and vigilant—but their eyes carried a timeless wisdom, a depth earned only by those who had witnessed the rise and fall of empires, the passing of entire generations.

As he looked at them, Santiago felt the familiar pang of both pride and sorrow, for he knew the cost of the vow they all carried. Their agelessness was not merely a gift; it was a binding tether, a symbol of their unyielding commitment to God and the Church. Bound by their oath, they would serve until their last breath, their lives devoted to a cause that transcended time.

The powers granted to the Iberian Guard were bestowed upon them during a solemn ceremony, one that each member remembered with reverence and awe. They were recruited young, chosen from among the most devout and capable, men and women who displayed unwavering faith and resilience even in the face of adversity. Only a select few—those who demonstrated not only skill but an unbreakable dedication to God—were brought into the fold.

As Santiago looked upon his comrades, memories of his own coronation ceremony stirred within him. He had been just thirty years old, a devout soldier who had already proven his loyalty through years of service. But the ceremony had been unlike anything he had imagined, a rite that went beyond physical endurance, beyond even the strongest of faiths. It was a transformation, one that bound his soul to the very essence of the Church.

The ritual had taken place deep within the Vatican's hidden catacombs, witnessed only by the highest clergy. Cloaked in silence and shadows, Santiago had knelt before the Pope, his heart pounding with both fear and reverence as the holy oil was placed upon his forehead, marking him as one of the chosen.

Pope Leo's words still echoed in his mind, as clear now as they had been on that fateful day. "By this anointing, you shall be bound to serve the Lord and His Church, timeless and unyielding. As you are now, so you shall remain, in strength, in youth, and in duty, until your last breath."

As the oil had seeped into his skin, Santiago had felt a warmth spreading through his body, a sensation both foreign and profound. It was as if his very being was being reshaped, remade in devotion to a purpose greater than himself. His vision had blurred, his pulse quickening as a strange energy took hold of him, filling him with strength, clarity, and an unbreakable resolve.

From that day forward, he and his fellow Guards had carried abilities that marked them as more than mortal. Their agility was heightened, their reflexes sharpened to a degree that defied natural limits. Their endurance surpassed that of ordinary men, allowing them to endure battles, missions, and hardships that would cripple others. And, most profound of all, they did not age. Their bodies, preserved in their prime, served as vessels of faith and duty, enduring through centuries without decay.

But these powers came with a cost, one that each Guard knew all too well. For as long as they served, they would be bound to the Church, their lives entwined with its fate. They could not grow old, could not die of natural causes, could not share in the lives of the mortal world that passed around them. Their existence was eternal, yet isolated, for they were set apart, chosen for a purpose that came before all else.

Santiago's thoughts returned to the present as he surveyed his comrades, each one a reflection of the same unbreakable vow. Isabela, their linguist and master of disguise, had been a young scholar before joining the Guard, her keen intellect matched only by her devotion. She had long since given up her life of study to serve the Church, her youth preserved, but her heart marked by the sacrifices she had made.

Marco, their silent sentinel, had been a man of faith from a young age, his steadfastness and strength as unyielding as the armor he wore. He had been raised in a remote village, trained as a soldier before being chosen by the Guard. Now, he stood as a warrior tempered by time, his body strong and agile, his mind focused on the mission that lay ahead.

Emmanuel, their expert in hand-to-hand combat, had once been a simple man, known for his quick reflexes and sharp wit. But his loyalty to the Church had led him to this path, and now he served with a quiet intensity that belied his agelessness.

And Rafael, their archer, had been a hunter before joining the Guard, his skill with the bow unmatched. He was a man of few words, yet his loyalty to the Church was unwavering, his aim as steady as his faith.

Santiago met their gazes, knowing that they, too, felt the weight of their duty. They shared an understanding that went beyond words—a bond forged not only by their shared powers, but by the sacrifices they had made, the lives they had left behind, and the timeless duty they had sworn to uphold.

Isabela broke the silence, her voice soft but filled with resolve. "It is strange, isn't it? To walk among the living yet remain untouched by time, to see lives pass as if they were mere shadows."

Santiago nodded, understanding her sentiment. "We are bound to this purpose, Isabela. It is a sacrifice we all accepted, knowing the cost."

She looked at him, her eyes reflecting both sorrow and determination. "Sometimes, I wonder if we are truly alive, or if we are merely vessels—tools fashioned for the Church, shaped by its hand."

Emmanuel stepped forward, placing a hand on her shoulder. "We live for something greater than ourselves, Isabela. 'The fear of the Lord is the beginning of wisdom,' as Solomon said. Our lives have meaning because we serve His purpose."

Isabela offered a faint smile, nodding in agreement. "'Trust in the Lord with all your heart and lean not on your own understanding,'" she quoted softly, drawing strength from the scripture.

Santiago felt a swell of pride as he looked upon his comrades. They had each borne the weight of their ageless existence, carrying their faith like a shield. But he knew that this mission would test them in ways they had not yet faced. The Viper and his Zealots represented not only a physical threat, but an ideological one—an enemy who sought to unravel the very faith they had devoted their lives to protect.

He spoke, his voice steady and resolute. "We are the guardians of the Church, bound by faith, preserved by our vow. We may walk unseen among men, but our purpose is eternal. Our mission is sacred, and we must not fail."

The Guard members exchanged solemn nods, their faces reflecting the determination and unity that defined their order. They knew that the path ahead would be treacherous, but they were ready to face it together, bound by their unyielding loyalty to God and the Church.

As they prepared for the journey ahead, Santiago felt a sense of peace settle over him. Their agelessness was both a gift and a curse, but it was one they bore willingly, for they understood that their lives were not their own. They were servants of the Church, guardians of the faith, and they would defend it with every breath, every ounce of strength, for as long as their vow endured.

In the dim light of the Guard's chamber, Santiago stood before his fellow Guards, his posture steady as he held the map the Pope had entrusted him with. His comrades watched him intently, their faces reflecting a mixture of solemn anticipation and quiet resolve. He could feel the tension in the air—the familiar silence before a mission, when words held weight and each glance conveyed more than a thousand spoken promises.

"Brothers and sister," Santiago began, his voice even, "we have been summoned to protect the Church, not only from an enemy that seeks to challenge its authority, but from a force that threatens the faith itself. The Pope has tasked us with retrieving the Codex Veritas before it can fall into the hands of the Zealots of Veritas. They believe this relic holds knowledge that could undermine the foundation of faith and fracture Christendom beyond repair."

He let the words settle, watching as his comrades absorbed the weight of their task. Each of them had faced peril before, fought battles and completed missions that required both skill and unwavering devotion. But this mission was unlike any they had undertaken. The Codex Veritas was not just a symbol—it was a weapon, and in the wrong hands, it could bring ruin.

"We leave for Germany at first light," he continued, unrolling the map for them to see. "The Pope's intelligence suggests the Codex is hidden in a monastery in the heart of Protestant territory. Our journey will take us across borders and into lands where the Church's influence has weakened. We will travel as pilgrims, blending in as best we can, but we must remain vigilant. The Viper's men are everywhere, and they know we're coming."

Rafael, ever the stoic archer, stepped forward, his gaze scanning the route Santiago had mapped out. "If they know we're coming, they'll anticipate our path. They'll have men watching every town, every market. We must be prepared to adapt and change our route as needed."

Santiago nodded, grateful for Rafael's foresight. "Agreed. Flexibility is key. We will use alternative paths whenever possible, and we will move under the cover of night to minimize our visibility."

Isabela leaned closer, studying the map with a critical eye. Her knowledge of languages and local customs made her indispensable in unfamiliar territory. "The towns we'll pass through are close to the heart of the Reformation. They will be wary of outsiders, especially those who appear tied to the Church. We must be careful not to draw attention. I can help with translations and dialects to blend in, but we'll need a story to explain our travels."

"We'll pose as a group of scholars," Santiago suggested, "pilgrims on a journey to collect relics for study. It is not uncommon, and it will explain our need to travel through remote regions. Isabela, you'll handle any questions or suspicions."

Isabela nodded, a flicker of pride in her eyes. "Understood. I'll make sure we are seen as curious scholars, nothing more."

Emmanuel, who had remained silent until now, stepped forward, his hands resting on the hilts of his twin short swords. "And if we encounter the Zealots of Veritas?" he asked, his voice low and calm. "They are not merely reformists—they are trained, armed, and committed to their cause."

The room fell silent as the others considered Emmanuel's words. The Zealots were known for their fanaticism, their belief that they were liberating people from the "chains" of faith. They would not hesitate to strike against anyone who threatened their mission.

"If we encounter them, we must avoid open confrontation," Santiago replied. "Our goal is to retrieve the Codex without drawing attention. Fighting will only delay us and put us at greater risk. But if there is no other choice, we will defend ourselves."

Marco, a man of few words but unbreakable loyalty, spoke up. "And what of the locals? The Pope said there are informants within the reformist ranks. Should we be wary of civilians as well?"

"Yes," Santiago said. "The Viper has spread his influence beyond the ranks of the Zealots. He has informants, spies, and sympathizers in many places. We will treat every stranger with caution."

Santiago paused, allowing the gravity of their mission to sink in. They were walking into a land of shifting loyalties, where every ally could be an enemy and every village a potential trap. Yet he trusted his team implicitly; they were more than soldiers—they were his brothers and sister in faith, bound by a vow that went beyond words.

As they discussed strategies, each Guard member contributed their unique expertise, weaving together a plan that balanced caution with precision. Rafael spoke of possible ambush sites along the route, drawing from his knowledge of terrain and tactics. Marco, ever the pragmatist, shared his insights on defensive formations, ways they could shield one another if attacked in close quarters.

Emmanuel, known for his skill in close combat, proposed tactics for disarming opponents quickly and quietly, reducing the chance of causing an uproar. He demonstrated a series of swift maneuvers with his twin short swords, his movements fluid and controlled.

Isabela, meanwhile, reviewed the cultural nuances of the regions they would traverse. She explained the dialects and customs they might encounter, the mannerisms they would need to adopt to avoid suspicion. Her linguistic expertise would be their first line of defense, a shield that would keep them hidden in plain sight.

Finally, Santiago addressed the emotional toll of the mission, knowing that each of them would face tests of faith and endurance. "This journey will not be easy. We will be walking through lands that have already begun to turn away from the Church. The Viper and his Zealots are spreading a poison that clouds the minds of the faithful, turning them against the very foundation of our beliefs."

He looked at each of his comrades, meeting their gazes. "We are here to protect the Church, to uphold the faith that has been entrusted to us. Remember the words of Proverbs: 'The fear of the Lord is the beginning of knowledge, but fools despise wisdom and instruction.' We are not fools. We are the guardians of that wisdom."

They nodded, their expressions solemn yet determined. The bond they shared was unspoken but unbreakable—a unity forged not only through battle, but through the countless years they had served together. They knew that their agelessness was a reminder of the life they had sacrificed for this cause, a life given to something greater than themselves.

Santiago continued, his voice softer now, yet filled with conviction. "We are the Iberian Guard. Our duty is eternal, as is our loyalty. This mission will test us in ways we may not yet understand, but we do not walk alone. We walk with faith as our guide, and with each other."

Emmanuel placed a steady hand on Santiago's shoulder, his gaze filled with unshakeable trust. "Then let us go, Captain, and let no man or force deter us from this path. We serve God, and no other."

The words seemed to carry a weight that resonated in the chamber, binding them all in shared purpose. They had prepared for countless missions before, but this time felt different—a mission that would test not only their skills but their devotion, their understanding of what it meant to serve a faith that endured beyond the bounds of mortality.

As they gathered their weapons and prepared their travel packs, Santiago felt a deep sense of peace settle over him. They were prepared. Their strategy was sound, their unity unshaken. Together, they would protect the Church, defend its relics, and safeguard the faith that so many depended upon.

As dawn broke over the Vatican, casting the first light over Rome, Santiago and his team moved silently through the hidden passageways, cloaked in the robes of pilgrims. Their armor was hidden beneath their cloaks, their weapons concealed but ready. They were the Iberian Guard, a force bound by faith and ageless loyalty, walking into the heart of danger for the sake of the Church.

In the dim glow, Santiago led them through the passages that would take them beyond the Vatican's protective walls. He felt the familiar weight of his mission settle over him, a reminder of the purpose that had defined his life for centuries. Around him, his comrades walked with quiet resolve, their footsteps soft against the stone floor, each step measured and deliberate.

As they reached the courtyard that opened into the outer streets, Santiago paused, turning to face his team. Isabela, Marco, Emmanuel, and Rafael gathered around him, their eyes reflecting the same quiet determination that Santiago felt within himself. They were the Church's most trusted guardians, an elite few who had pledged their lives to the faith, unyielding and unbreakable.

"From here on, we are pilgrims," Santiago said, his voice low yet firm. "Our path will be treacherous, but we move with purpose. Remember, our mission is not just to secure the Codex but to protect the faith that so many hold dear. We are the guardians of that faith, and we walk with God's strength."

His words seemed to resonate in the still morning air, settling over each member like a mantle of protection. He knew the road to Germany would be long, the journey perilous, and their enemies relentless. But he also knew the strength of the Guard, the unwavering loyalty that bound them together.

Emmanuel nodded, his face solemn. "And if we encounter the Zealots?"

"We avoid conflict whenever possible," Santiago replied. "We are not here to draw attention. But if there is no other choice, we will defend ourselves and each other. We proceed with caution, for we walk among those who would see the Church torn apart."

The others nodded, understanding the balance they would need to maintain between secrecy and strength. They were more than soldiers—they were guardians of faith, bound by a code that transcended time and demanded both restraint and conviction.

Isabela adjusted her cloak, her gaze steady. "Our path may be hidden from the eyes of man, but it is clear in the eyes of God."

Santiago offered a faint smile, feeling the strength of their shared purpose. "Then let us begin."

As they stepped out into the early morning light, the city of Rome lay quiet around them. They moved through narrow streets and alleyways, blending into the shadows, passing unnoticed by the few citizens stirring at this hour. In their pilgrim garb, they appeared to be nothing more than humble travelers, seeking holy relics in distant lands—a guise that concealed the deadly skills and weapons each of them bore.

The route to Germany was one they had studied carefully. They would travel by foot and, where necessary, by cart, following paths less traveled to avoid the main roads. Every detail had been meticulously planned, every step calculated to ensure they remained unseen. The disguise of pilgrims would serve them well, allowing them to pass through towns and villages without drawing suspicion. Isabela's knowledge of local dialects and customs would be invaluable, allowing them to blend into the crowds, to slip by unnoticed.

As they moved northward, leaving the familiar streets of Rome behind, Santiago could feel the weight of anticipation building within him. He knew that the journey ahead would test not only their skills but their loyalty, their faith, and their resolve. The Codex Veritas was a prize that many sought, a relic shrouded in myth and danger, and it was a testament to the Pope's trust in them that he had entrusted this mission to the Iberian Guard.

The road ahead stretched long and uncertain, a winding path that would take them through lands where the Church's influence had begun to fade, where reformists preached doctrines that challenged the very foundation of their faith. Santiago could feel the tension in the air, the sense that they were walking into a land divided, a land where enemies could be hidden in plain sight.

As they crossed the city's boundary, Santiago felt a pull within him, a quiet voice that reminded him of the timeless duty he carried. He paused, turning to his comrades, his voice carrying a note of both warning and encouragement.

"We may be stepping into the unknown," he said, "but we do not walk alone. As Proverbs reminds us, 'In all your ways acknowledge Him, and He shall direct your paths.' We are guided not only by our skills but by our faith. We are the Iberian Guard, bound by an oath that is unbreakable, and no force will deter us from our path."

The others nodded, their faces reflecting the same unwavering resolve. Isabela, her eyes bright with determination, stepped forward. "Wherever this journey leads, we go with faith as our guide."

Emmanuel raised his hand in silent agreement. "We are here to serve, Captain, to defend the faith. Let our mission be our testament."

Santiago felt a swell of pride as he looked upon his comrades. They had each sacrificed much to be here, had given their lives to a purpose that transcended time and mortality. Their ageless existence, a gift and a curse, was a reminder of the lives they had left behind, the families they could never return to, the world that moved on without them.

But he knew that none of them would have chosen otherwise. Their lives were devoted to something greater, a calling that bound them together in purpose and faith. And as they began their journey, Santiago felt a quiet certainty settle over him—a sense that whatever lay ahead, they were prepared to face it, bound by the unbreakable vow that defined them.

As they walked, the sun rose higher, casting a warm glow over the road ahead. The world around them seemed to come alive, the distant sounds of morning filling the air—the chirping of birds, the rustling of leaves, the soft murmur of wind through the trees. It was a peaceful scene, yet Santiago knew that beneath this tranquility lay a deeper tension, a sense of conflict that rippled through the land they walked upon.

They passed through small villages, their cloaks pulled low, moving swiftly and silently. In each town, Isabela spoke with the locals, her knowledge of languages and customs smoothing their passage. She adopted the role of a humble scholar, speaking with an accent that matched the local dialects, blending into the fabric of each place they visited. With her guidance, they moved unnoticed, a group of humble pilgrims journeying through a land of unrest.

As they traveled, Santiago found himself reflecting on the journey they had undertaken. It was not just a mission to retrieve a relic; it was a mission to protect the faith that had sustained countless generations, a faith that was now under siege from within and without. The Codex Veritas was more than a mere artifact—it was a symbol, a testament to the power of belief and the dangers that lurked when that belief was challenged.

With each step they took, Santiago felt the weight of their task pressing upon him, a reminder of the timeless duty they carried. They were not just soldiers; they were guardians of a faith that spanned centuries, protectors of a legacy that had shaped the lives of millions. And as they walked into the unknown, he felt a quiet strength within him—a resolve that nothing could shake.

As the sun climbed higher, casting its light over the path ahead, Santiago offered one final prayer, a silent vow to protect the faith, to guard the relic that held such profound significance. And as he looked upon his comrades, he knew that they, too, carried this same vow, a promise bound by the very essence of their existence.

Together, they walked into the dawn, a force bound by faith, ready to face whatever dangers awaited them on the road to Germany. For they were the Iberian Guard, timeless and unyielding, and they would defend the Church with every breath, every step, until the end.

**Chapter 2: Into Hostile Territory**

The landscape around them shifted gradually as the Iberian Guard crossed into German territory. Rolling hills and deep forests replaced the familiar Italian countryside, the road winding through dense woods and open fields dotted with isolated farmhouses. The air felt colder, the sky more somber under a layer of shifting gray clouds. Santiago glanced at the distant horizon, feeling a strange sense of foreboding settle over him.

As they moved northward, he sensed the change in atmosphere, a palpable tension that seemed to hang over the villages and small towns they passed. This was no longer the Rome he knew—a city firmly anchored in tradition, where faith wove through the lives of its people, tangible and unchallenged. Here, they had entered a land where faith had begun to fracture, where reformist ideas had taken root, sowing doubt and dissent.

The Guard kept their pace steady, cloaked in their pilgrim robes, their hoods drawn low. Though they were in disguise, each of them felt the subtle shift in mood as they encountered the locals along the way. People stared longer, faces drawn and guarded, eyes narrowed with suspicion or curiosity. Few spoke to them, and those who did offered only curt nods or distracted glances, as though wary of any connection to strangers.

Walking beside Santiago, Emmanuel's sharp gaze swept over the village, lingering on each passerby. His usual calm was edged with tension. "It's a strange feeling, Captain. These people see us, but they don't *see* us. There's a wariness in their eyes."

Santiago nodded. "Yes. There's a chill here that goes beyond the weather. These people are no longer looking to the Church for answers—they've been drawn into something else."

"Feels almost as though we're among enemies," Marco murmured, one hand resting near the hilt of his sword.

Emmanuel shook his head, a faint frown creasing his brow. "Not quite enemies. But they look at us with the eyes of those who no longer trust. Faith doesn't unite them as it does us. It divides them. They feel divided."

Rafael, ever vigilant, walked a few paces behind them, his gaze flicking over the passersby, watching for any sign of danger. "They seem as though they're hiding something. It's more than curiosity."

"They are," Santiago replied. "They're hiding their allegiance. It may not be open, but they're questioning the Church, doubting its authority. We're walking through lands where loyalty is no longer assured."

As they moved forward, Isabela lowered her voice. "Luther's words have a hold here, a powerful one. The Church may have to contend with this sooner than we thought."

Emmanuel sighed, his tone contemplative. "The Reformation has spread quickly, it seems. These symbols"—he motioned to the ash marks discreetly painted on certain doors—"are not a coincidence. They are public and bold, reminders that a shift has occurred here, one that is spreading beyond these borders."

They passed through a small village, and a few wary children peered out from behind a fence. An older woman met their gaze with a guarded look, offering a small loaf of bread to Santiago. He accepted it graciously, blessing her, though she turned away without a word. Santiago felt Emmanuel's watchful presence beside him, a steady reminder that they were not alone in this foreign land, though it felt increasingly as if the people's hearts and minds were far removed from their mission.

The Guard continued on, passing through the village and onto a narrow trail that wound through a dense forest. The path was well-worn, though mostly empty save for a few travelers who passed by without so much as a glance. The trees cast long shadows across the ground, their branches forming a canopy that shielded them from the morning light. It was a quiet place, but Santiago felt the tension in the air, a sense that even the land itself was caught in the unrest that stirred its people.

After a time, Emmanuel broke the silence. "These people don't see us as protectors, Captain. To them, we're outsiders—maybe even enemies. To fulfill this mission, we may need to become invisible."

Santiago nodded. "It's true. We're not just walking into foreign land—we're walking into a place where the very foundation of faith has been shaken. These people may no longer look to the Church for guidance, and that makes them dangerous."

Rafael adjusted his bow under his cloak, his expression grim. "We'll have to be on constant guard. If they suspect we're here on Church business, they could turn against us in an instant."

"They could," Santiago agreed. "But remember, we are here to protect the faith, even if these people have forgotten its worth. Our mission is to secure the Codex and prevent it from falling into hands that would misuse it. Whatever distrust or hostility we face, we must remain focused."

Emmanuel's expression darkened as he glanced back at the village they had left behind. "Faith should be a comfort, a guiding force, yet here, it's become a source of division. We may find ourselves walking through shadows for the remainder of our mission."

Isabela looked over at Emmanuel, her voice softening. "It's strange, isn't it? To see people turn away from what once brought them hope. Faith was the thread that held communities together, and now it's being torn apart."

Emmanuel met her gaze, his tone unwavering. "It's our duty to remember the strength in faith, even if they can't. These symbols, these signs—they may give the people courage, but they are temporary. They lack the permanence of true faith, the bond that we share."

Santiago placed a steadying hand on Isabela's shoulder. "Faith is still here, Isabela. It may be hidden, buried beneath doubt and anger, but it remains. It is up to us to protect it, to ensure that it survives this storm."

They walked in silence for a time, each of them lost in their own thoughts. Santiago's mind drifted to the people of these villages, to the woman who had given them bread, to the children whose laughter had been stilled by the weight of doubt. He knew that the Codex Veritas represented more than just knowledge—it was a testament to the faith that had endured for centuries, a relic of a truth that went beyond words and doctrines.

Emmanuel, walking beside him, seemed to sense the heaviness in Santiago's thoughts. "Captain, remember that faith is our shield, and the Lord is our fortress. We are called to protect that which many have forsaken. We will see this mission through."

Santiago offered a silent prayer, asking for guidance, for strength, for the resolve to complete their mission no matter the cost. They were walking into a land of shadows, a place where trust had withered, and belief had been questioned. But they were the Iberian Guard, bound by a vow that was as timeless as the faith they served.

Their journey had only just begun, and Santiago knew that the road ahead would be filled with trials. But as he looked upon his comrades, he felt a sense of quiet certainty—a reminder that they did not walk this path alone. Together, they would face the darkness, for they were bound by a duty that transcended borders and beliefs, an oath that could not be shaken by the doubts of men.

And as they moved deeper into Germany, the sky darkening above them, they felt the weight of that duty settle over them like a mantle of purpose, guiding them forward into the unknown.

The village of Waldheim lay nestled in a small valley, its timber-framed houses lined with thatched roofs and small, carefully tended gardens. Smoke rose from chimneys as morning fires were stoked, filling the air with a faint haze. Despite the quaint charm of the place, Santiago felt the ever-present tension that clung to the town. It was in the wary eyes of villagers, the low murmurs that ceased when they passed, the way people seemed to keep to themselves, watching strangers from a safe distance.

The Guard approached the village carefully, with Santiago, Isabela, and Emmanuel at the forefront, while the others kept to the shadows nearby, ready to intervene if needed. Their pilgrim garb helped them blend in, casting them as simple travelers, though Santiago's sharp gaze missed nothing. Emmanuel, too, had donned a quiet demeanor, but his eyes scanned the village with a mixture of caution and curiosity, attuned to any hint of hostility.

"Remember," Santiago said, his voice low as he glanced toward Isabela, "we're here to gather information, not to make enemies. The Codex's location is our priority, but we need to tread carefully. These people have no reason to trust us."

Isabela nodded, her face obscured beneath her hood, though her eyes gleamed with determination. "I understand. I'll approach them carefully—let them see us as humble travelers, nothing more."

Emmanuel, standing on Santiago's other side, gave a slight nod, his voice calm but purposeful. "I'll keep an eye out for anyone who seems suspicious. If the Viper's influence runs deep here, his men may be watching us even now."

"Agreed," Santiago replied, acknowledging Emmanuel's caution with a nod. "We'll all need to be on guard."

The first task was to find a common gathering place, somewhere they could quietly listen and observe. As they moved through the narrow streets, Santiago noted the villagers watching from doorways and windows, their expressions guarded. They passed a small chapel, its stone walls faded with age, and he couldn't help but notice that it looked worn and neglected. Even the cross that hung above the entrance was tarnished, a subtle sign of the town's waning allegiance to the Church.

Ahead, a modest tavern sat at the edge of the square. Its sign, painted with the image of a stag, swayed slightly in the breeze. From within, the sound of low voices and clinking mugs could be heard. Santiago gestured for Isabela and

Emmanuel to follow him, and they entered the dimly lit establishment.

The tavern's patrons were few—a handful of men seated at rough-hewn tables, each one engrossed in his drink or conversation. They cast suspicious glances at Santiago, Isabela, and Emmanuel, but their curiosity quickly faded as Isabela greeted them in fluent German, her voice soft and unassuming.

"Good day, gentlemen," she said, offering a small smile as she moved to the bar. "We are travelers on pilgrimage, and we've come seeking rest and a bit of guidance. This is unfamiliar land to us."

The innkeeper, a man with a grizzled beard and weary eyes, nodded, his gaze lingering on her with a mixture of interest and caution. "A pilgrimage, you say?" he replied in German, his voice rough but polite. "Not many pilgrims passing through these days. Folk keep to themselves."

Isabela nodded, casting a subtle glance at Santiago before continuing. "We've heard as much," she replied, her tone respectful. "But we are compelled by faith, and our journey takes us through this region. We've also heard there are old relics and sites of interest in these lands. Perhaps you could help us?"

The innkeeper hesitated, his gaze shifting to Santiago, who kept his expression neutral. Emmanuel, sensing the man's lingering suspicion, leaned in slightly, adding in a calm tone, "We mean no trouble, sir. We only seek knowledge to deepen our faith, to see the holy sites that we've heard of."

At this, the innkeeper seemed to relax slightly, though a hint of caution remained in his eyes. "Well, I suppose there are still a few relics around," he said slowly. "Though I don't know what good they do. Times are changing. People have other concerns these days—faith is for those who have little else to worry about."

Isabela leaned forward, her voice barely above a whisper, drawing the man's attention. "And yet... we've heard there may be a relic of great importance nearby. A tome that holds wisdom passed down through the ages."

The innkeeper's gaze sharpened, and he studied her carefully, as if weighing her words. Santiago noted the shift in the man's demeanor—a mixture of interest and wariness, as though he understood exactly what she was referring to but was unsure whether he should speak of it.

"Wisdom, you say?" he muttered, casting a quick glance around the tavern. "There's talk of such things... though I wouldn't go asking too loudly. Not everyone here takes kindly to those kinds of questions."

"Then we'll tread carefully," Isabela replied, her tone gentle. "But we would be grateful for any guidance you might offer. We have traveled far, and our purpose is to honor and protect what we seek."

The innkeeper considered this, his expression softening. "If you must know," he murmured, leaning closer, "there's talk of a monastery a few miles north of here. Old place, mostly empty now. They say it was once a center of knowledge... might be what you're looking for."

Emmanuel, who had remained silent until now, offered a respectful nod. "Thank you, sir. We'll keep your advice close to heart. It is a blessing to meet those willing to share the road's wisdom."

The innkeeper straightened, his expression turning cautious once more. "Be careful, strangers. Not everyone here will take kindly to your search. There are those who see such relics as symbols of a past they'd rather forget."

Santiago noted the warning in the man's tone and the implication that reformist sentiments ran deep in this village. The Codex, it seemed, was not merely a relic but a symbol of the faith that many here had abandoned, a reminder of a Church they no longer followed.

With a quiet word of thanks, Santiago, Isabela, and Emmanuel left the tavern, stepping back into the village square. The morning sun had climbed higher, casting a pale light over the rooftops. Around them, villagers went about their routines, though their eyes lingered a bit too long on the Guard members as they walked through the square.

They moved in silence, exchanging only brief glances as they walked through the narrow streets, their steps unhurried yet purposeful. Santiago could feel the weight of their discovery settling over them, a mixture of hope and tension. They had a destination, but it was clear that reaching it would be no simple task.

"Do you think he was telling the truth?" Emmanuel asked once they were out of earshot, his voice low but thoughtful.

Santiago nodded, his gaze thoughtful. "I believe so. But I also believe he knows more than he's letting on. The way he spoke—it was as though he knew the Codex was significant, but he feared speaking of it openly."

"Perhaps the reformist influence is stronger here than we thought," Isabela suggested. "If the villagers see the Codex as a symbol of the Church's authority, they may view anyone who seeks it with suspicion... or hostility."

Santiago's jaw tightened. "Then we'll proceed with caution. We have our lead, but we must be vigilant. The Viper's influence is likely to be strong here, and if his men know of the Codex, they will be watching for anyone who shows interest in it."

As they walked through the village, they passed a small chapel, its doors partially open. Santiago caught a glimpse of its worn interior—the simple altar, the faded paintings, the empty pews. It was a reminder of the faith that had once united this place, a faith now fractured and weakened by doubt and dissent.

Isabela's gaze lingered on the chapel as they walked by, a flicker of sadness crossing her face. "It is strange, isn't it? To see a place once dedicated to faith left abandoned. As if they've turned their backs on something that was once sacred."

Emmanuel placed a steadying hand on her shoulder. "Faith endures, Isabela. Even here, even among those who doubt. We must protect what remains, even if they have forgotten its worth."

Santiago looked at his comrades, feeling a quiet determination settle within him. They were entering a land where trust was a rare commodity, where faith was no longer a shared bond but a source of division. But they were the Iberian Guard, bound by an oath that transcended borders and beliefs.

And as they moved toward the distant hills where the monastery lay hidden, he felt a renewed sense of purpose—a reminder that their mission was not just to retrieve a relic, but to protect a faith that had endured for centuries.

The Guard moved cautiously into the larger town of Badenberg, its market square bustling with villagers, merchants, and travelers. Here, the air was thick with the sounds of bargaining and laughter, though Santiago sensed an undercurrent of tension running through the crowd. Stalls filled with fresh produce, bolts of cloth, and assorted trinkets surrounded them, forming a maze of colors and noise that concealed as much as it revealed.

As they navigated the square, Santiago gestured for his team to spread out slightly, each taking different routes through the crowd. The plan was to blend in, to observe quietly without drawing attention, while keeping an eye on any hint of reformist activity. They wore their hoods low and kept their movements casual, their demeanor mirroring that of weary travelers just passing through.

Isabela walked a few paces ahead of Santiago, stopping at a cloth vendor's stall and engaging the seller in polite conversation, her voice lilting in German with a practiced accent. She laughed softly, asking questions about the cloth's origins, her manner friendly and warm. Santiago knew this approach would help to build trust, to make them appear harmless, inconspicuous.

Meanwhile, Emmanuel took a route to the opposite side of the square, his eyes scanning the crowd with calm vigilance. His posture was that of a casual traveler, but Santiago knew that Emmanuel's every sense was attuned to danger, alert for any signs of suspicion or hostility. As he passed a spice merchant's stall, Emmanuel subtly adjusted his hood to keep his face obscured, allowing him to observe the square without drawing attention.

Santiago's gaze shifted, picking out subtle details in the crowd—the way certain individuals lingered just a little too long, their gazes sliding away the moment they felt his glance. These men didn't look like typical townsfolk; they held themselves with a quiet intensity, their postures tense, their expressions alert.

He noted three of them, each stationed at different points around the square. They were too scattered to be a group of travelers and too focused to be ordinary villagers. As he watched, one of them—an older man with a rough beard and narrow eyes—leaned close to a nearby vendor and whispered something. The vendor nodded, casting a furtive glance in Santiago's direction before continuing his work.

Emmanuel caught Santiago's gaze from across the square, a faint signal of understanding passing between them. He subtly moved closer, positioning himself to maintain a clear line of sight to Santiago and Isabela, ready to intervene if needed.

"Reformist spies," Santiago murmured to Isabela, his tone neutral as he observed the men. "Three of them, near the edge of the square. They're watching anyone who doesn't look like a local. We need to avoid drawing attention, but they'll keep watching us if we stay in one place."

Isabela nodded, her expression unchanging as she adjusted her hood to shadow her face further. "Perhaps we should split up. I could move toward the market's other side, divert their attention."

"No," Santiago replied. "Stay close. They'll be watching for any signs of separation. If they suspect we're avoiding them, it will only increase their suspicion."

Just then, Emmanuel approached, his arrival silent but timely. He had already assessed the situation, his gaze flicking over the reformist spies as he joined Santiago and Isabela, his expression composed.

"They're watching more than just us," he murmured, glancing around. "It looks like they have people stationed at the exits as well. They're casting a net, trying to control who leaves."

Santiago's jaw tightened. This wasn't just casual observation; it was an organized effort to monitor outsiders and potentially detain anyone who aroused suspicion. The reformist network here was well-organized, more extensive than he'd anticipated.

"Then we'll need to leave without giving them reason to follow," Santiago said, his tone calm but resolute. "Stay close, keep moving. Act as though we're simply passing through."

They made their way toward the opposite side of the square, moving with deliberate slowness, as though browsing the market wares without any particular destination in mind. Santiago noted that the spies continued to watch, their gazes trailing after them with calculated interest. He knew that if they couldn't evade suspicion soon, a confrontation would be inevitable.

As they reached a stall selling leather goods, Isabela stopped, picking up a small pouch and examining it thoughtfully. Her demeanor was casual, her expression one of mild curiosity, but her eyes held a glint of alertness as she scanned the nearby crowd. Santiago, meanwhile, turned his attention to a rack of belts, feigning interest as he kept the spies within his peripheral vision.

One of the spies—a man with a scar running across his left eyebrow—was edging closer, pretending to inspect a cart laden with barrels. Santiago watched him carefully, noting the man's hand resting just a little too close to his dagger, his stance ready, as though he anticipated trouble.

Santiago leaned closer to Emmanuel and Isabela, his voice barely audible. "If they move any closer, we'll be forced to act. Keep your weapons concealed, but stay ready."

Emmanuel's hand brushed against his cloak, his fingers instinctively finding the grip of his dagger. "Understood. But if it comes to a confrontation, we'll need to draw them away from the square. We can't afford to make a scene here."

Suddenly, another of the spies—a wiry, quick-eyed man—moved toward them, his expression hardening as he approached. He positioned himself within earshot, his gaze flicking over each of them, assessing them with a thinly veiled hostility.

"Travelers, are you?" he said, his tone sharp, the faint hint of suspicion curling through his words. "Not many pilgrims pass through here these days."

Isabela turned to him, her face composed, offering a polite smile. "Yes, indeed. We are journeying northward, following the path of old saints and relics. We mean no harm—just humble pilgrims seeking spiritual nourishment."

The man's expression remained distrustful, his eyes narrowing slightly. "Strange, isn't it, that pilgrims would find their way to this part of the world, especially in these times?"

Emmanuel sensed the rising tension and stepped forward, offering a calm but steady gaze. "Faith has no boundaries, my friend," he said in a measured tone. "Sometimes the journey itself leads us to places we did not expect. We seek only to honor the saints and pass through in peace."

The spy's eyes lingered on Emmanuel's face, searching for any hint of deception. Emmanuel met his gaze with unwavering calm, his expression one of quiet sincerity. After a moment, the man let out a grunt, though his suspicion remained evident.

"Faith," the man muttered. "A noble thing, I suppose. But here, faith has taken on a new form. Be careful, travelers. There are those who don't take kindly to strangers—especially those who seem to be holding onto old beliefs."

With that, the man turned and walked away, his gaze still fixed on them as he joined the other spies, murmuring something under his breath.

Santiago felt a surge of relief, though he remained alert, his senses heightened as he watched the man retreat. The encounter had left an impression, a mark of suspicion that would follow them if they lingered.

"We need to leave," he said quietly. "They're suspicious, but they haven't acted yet. If we're lucky, we can slip away before they decide to follow."

Isabela, Emmanuel, and Rafael nodded, and together, they began moving toward the nearest exit. They maintained their calm demeanor, each of them casting subtle glances over their shoulders as they made their way through the crowd. The reformist spies watched, but made no further move, content to observe from a distance.

As they reached the edge of the square, Santiago's gaze met that of the scarred spy, a silent acknowledgment passing between them—a warning that this encounter was far from over. He knew that these men were unlikely to forget the presence of strangers, especially ones who had aroused even the slightest suspicion.

The Guard moved through the narrow streets leading out of the town, their footsteps quiet as they slipped into the outskirts. They maintained their steady pace until they were beyond the village boundaries, far enough to avoid immediate pursuit.

Once they were certain they were alone, Emmanuel spoke, his voice steady but carrying an edge of frustration. "The reformists have eyes everywhere. Even if we're careful, we'll be under constant watch."

Santiago nodded, his expression grave. "This won't be the last encounter. The Viper's network reaches farther than we thought. From now on, we must assume that every town, every village has informants."

Isabela looked back toward the town, her face thoughtful. "If they're so organized, the Codex must be more significant than we realized. We're not just retrieving a relic—we're facing an entire movement."

Santiago placed a hand on her shoulder, his gaze filled with resolve. "Then we will proceed carefully. Our mission remains the same, but our approach must adapt. We are not here to fight a war; we are here to protect what is sacred. We move with caution, we blend in, and we do not give them a reason to remember us."

They shared a silent agreement, each of them feeling the weight of their task settle over them anew. The reformist movement was strong, perhaps even stronger than they had anticipated, but the Iberian Guard had faced dangers before. Their purpose was clear, their loyalty unwavering.

With one last look around the town, Santiago led his team onward, their path now shrouded in the shadow of unseen eyes, each step carrying them deeper into the heart of hostile territory.

The sun had begun its slow descent by the time the Guard reached the outskirts of Badenberg, the light casting a golden glow over the distant hills. Following a faint path through the woods, Santiago led the group toward a small clearing, where a cluster of stone ruins sat quietly among the trees. The area was deserted, its solitude almost eerie, but there was a sense of purpose in the quiet place that drew Santiago forward.

They were here to meet with a man known as Brother Jakob, a monk who had chosen to live in seclusion, away from the rising unrest that gripped the region. The monk had been mentioned by the innkeeper they'd spoken with earlier—a name dropped in hushed tones, as though speaking it too loudly might summon unwanted attention. Brother Jakob was rumored to know the local lore well, and he possessed knowledge that could prove valuable to the Guard's mission.

Santiago's gaze flickered over his team, each member alert and ready for whatever lay ahead. Emmanuel moved up beside Santiago, his presence solid and reassuring. He kept a hand on the hilt of his blade beneath his cloak, his stance alert, ready to act at the slightest hint of danger. He exchanged a quick nod with Santiago, silently reaffirming his readiness to support and protect. Emmanuel's sense of quiet fortitude brought a subtle comfort to the group, knowing he would be prepared for any outcome.

Moving with practiced silence, they made their way to the ruins, weaving through the shadows cast by the crumbling stone walls. As they neared the remains of what might once have been a small chapel, a figure stepped from the shadows, cloaked in a simple robe that nearly blended with the stone around him. The man's face was thin and worn, his eyes sharp and cautious. He watched the Guard approach, a faint trace of wariness evident in his stance, but he did not retreat.

"Are you Brother Jakob?" Santiago asked, his voice steady yet respectful.

The monk inclined his head, studying Santiago and his companions with a calculating gaze. His eyes rested on Emmanuel, whose calm and resolute demeanor seemed to put him at ease. "I am. And you are strangers... yet not entirely unfamiliar." His gaze lingered on the cross embroidered on Santiago's collar. "You are men of faith, yet your presence here carries a heavier purpose."

Santiago nodded. "We are pilgrims, seeking truth in these uncertain times. But we have come to you in need of guidance."

The monk's lips curved in a faint smile, his expression tinged with a strange mix of understanding and resignation. "Truth. A precious thing, indeed. Yet dangerous to those who cling to it too tightly." He gestured for them to follow him, leading them to a secluded alcove where they could speak without fear of being overheard.

As they settled, Brother Jakob spoke in a low voice, his tone laced with both reverence and caution. "I have heard whispers of why you are here, of the relic you seek. They call it the Codex Veritas—a tome of knowledge and wisdom, hidden for centuries. But you must understand, this is no ordinary text. The Codex is a symbol, a beacon of faith, yet it is also a temptation that has drawn many to ruin."

Isabela leaned forward, her eyes fixed on the monk. "We understand its significance, Brother Jakob. But we must protect it from those who would misuse it. Can you tell us where it might be found?"

The monk's expression grew pensive, his gaze drifting over the trees that surrounded them, as though searching for unseen watchers among the shadows. "There is a monastery," he said finally, his voice barely above a whisper. "An ancient place, hidden deep within the hills to the north. It was once a sanctuary for scholars and monks, a place where knowledge was preserved in secrecy."

"Is it still occupied?" Rafael asked, his tone cautious.

Brother Jakob shook his head. "Not for many years. The monastery was abandoned, its inhabitants scattered. But the records remain, hidden within its walls. It was there that the Codex was last kept, safeguarded by those who believed its wisdom should be shared only with those who were worthy. Yet... I fear that others have learned of its location."

Emmanuel's jaw tightened as he processed the monk's words. "Then time is against us. If the reformists seek the Codex, we must reach it before they do," he said, his voice steady, with a trace of urgency. His calm resolve served as a grounding force, balancing the gravity of the situation with the discipline required to face it.

"Tell us, Brother Jakob," Santiago said, his voice firm. "What dangers lie within this monastery? If the Codex is as powerful as you say, surely there are measures in place to protect it."

The monk's face grew solemn, his eyes darkening with the weight of what he was about to reveal. "The monastery is protected, yes. Its guardians were wise, and they foresaw the challenges that the Codex might bring. There are wards within its walls, traps designed to deter those who would seek it with ill intent. Only one who understands its purpose—who approaches with true faith—can hope to retrieve it."

The monk's gaze lingered on each member of the Guard, particularly Emmanuel, as though weighing the strength of their purpose. "But you must be careful. The Codex is not just a book; it is a repository of beliefs, a mirror that reflects the heart of those who seek it. For those who are unworthy, it reveals only illusions, leading them astray. Many have sought it, yet few have succeeded."

Emmanuel, feeling the gravity of the monk's words, spoke quietly. "We are bound by a higher calling, Brother Jakob. Our mission is to serve, to protect the sacred, even if it costs us our lives. Whatever trials await us, we face them willingly."

The monk nodded, respect in his eyes. "Then may your faith guide you. You must understand, though—the Codex is not only sought by reformists. There is another force at work—one that goes beyond the reformists. There is a group, a sect hidden in darkness, who believe the Codex holds the key to ancient powers. They are ruthless, driven by a desire for control that knows no bounds. They call themselves the Zealots of Veritas, and their reach is vast."

The name hung in the air like a poison. Emmanuel exchanged a grim look with Santiago, understanding the weight of this revelation. They had encountered the Zealots of Veritas's influence before, but the thought of such a powerful group pursuing the Codex heightened the urgency of their mission.

"The Zealots of Veritas" Santiago murmured, his voice tense. "We have crossed paths with their agents before. If they seek the Codex, then our mission has become even more urgent."

Brother Jakob nodded, his expression grave. "You understand now. The Codex is a beacon to those who crave power, and the Zealots of Veritas will stop at nothing to obtain it. They see it not as a source of wisdom, but as a tool—a means to control the minds and hearts of men."

Santiago placed a reassuring hand on the monk's shoulder, his voice filled with quiet conviction. "Your silence has preserved it thus far, Brother Jakob. Now it is our duty to protect it, to ensure that it does not fall into hands that would use it for harm."

The monk met Santiago's gaze, his expression softening with a hint of gratitude. "Then go, with my blessing. The monastery lies beyond the hills, hidden from plain sight. But be warned— The Zealots of Veritas' agents are cunning, and they may already be watching."

With one last nod of gratitude, Santiago and his team prepared to leave, the weight of their mission settling over them anew. They knew now that their journey would not be easy, that they would face both physical and spiritual challenges in the days to come. The Codex was more than a relic; it was a legacy, a symbol of the faith that had endured for centuries.

As they left the clearing, Emmanuel cast a final glance over his shoulder, watching as Brother Jakob faded into the shadows of the ruins, his form merging with the stones and trees around him. Emmanuel felt the responsibility settle over him—a charge not just to retrieve the Codex, but to guard its significance.

The Guard moved in silence, each of them lost in thought as they made their way toward the hills. Emmanuel's mind lingered on the monk's words, feeling the weight of his purpose renewed. Their mission was not merely to seek knowledge, but to protect the legacy of faith itself.

Ahead, the monastery awaited, hidden within the folds of the hills, its secrets guarded by time and faith. And Emmanuel knew they were ready, united in purpose, prepared to face whatever awaited them in the shadows of this divided land.

The sun dipped below the horizon, casting the village into shadow. A thin mist rolled in from the forest, veiling the town in a cloak of twilight. The Guard, their figures obscured in the fading light, moved quickly but quietly, weaving their way through narrow alleyways and side streets. Every footstep, every shadow seemed to carry the weight of danger, an unspoken warning that their presence had not gone unnoticed.

Santiago led the way, his gaze sharp and alert, scanning for any sign of movement among the villagers. He knew they couldn't afford to linger; their encounter with Brother Jakob had left them with valuable information, but it had also increased the risk of exposure. Suspicion brewed easily in places like this, where strangers were met with wary eyes and secrets lay buried beneath everyday routines.

As they passed a small cluster of houses, Santiago noticed a figure standing in the doorway of one of the cottages, watching them with an unsettling intensity. The man's gaze followed them as they moved, his hand resting on the hilt of a small knife tucked into his belt. Santiago met the man's gaze briefly before shifting his focus forward, signaling to the rest of the team to keep moving.

Emmanuel, positioned just behind Santiago, glanced back at the silent watcher, his eyes narrowing. He kept a steady hand near his dagger, ready to intervene if needed. In his presence, the Guard felt an additional layer of assurance, knowing Emmanuel's vigilance could make the difference in a quick escape or a dangerous encounter.

"Captain," Isabela whispered as she came up beside Santiago, her voice barely audible. "They're watching us. More than before."

"I know," Santiago replied, his voice a low murmur. "Our presence is drawing attention, and not the kind we want. We need to be swift and silent if we're to make it out of here unnoticed."

Rafael, ever watchful, took up the rear, his hand hovering close to his dagger, ready to respond if the situation turned. Emmanuel cast a quick glance toward Rafael, and a silent understanding passed between them—they were prepared to shield the team, whatever it took.

"Do you think they suspect we're here for the Codex?" Rafael asked quietly.

"Not yet," Santiago said, glancing back at the shadowed faces watching from the doorways and windows. "But they know we don't belong here, and that alone is enough to make them suspicious."

As they neared the edge of the village, Santiago heard a low murmur ripple through the crowd gathered near the central square. Word of strangers always spread fast in places like this, and he sensed the energy in the air shifting from curiosity to something darker—suspicion, perhaps even hostility.

Their steps quickened, but as they approached the narrow road leading out of town, Santiago noticed a group of men gathering by the path. They spoke in hushed tones, casting furtive glances in the Guard's direction. One of them, a tall man with a worn leather jacket and a scowl etched across his face, seemed to nod toward them, as if instructing the others.

"They're blocking the road," Marco muttered, his hand inching toward the sword concealed beneath his cloak. "They're not going to let us leave without questions."

Santiago quickly assessed their options. Confrontation would draw even more attention, something they couldn't afford. Their mission demanded subtlety and discretion, and a fight would only risk their cover. He turned to his team, his voice calm but firm.

"Follow me," he whispered, veering away from the main path and leading them down a narrow alley between two cottages. Emmanuel took up the flank, his movements steady and measured, ensuring no one was left behind or exposed. The alley wound toward the outskirts of the village, weaving through abandoned buildings and underbrush. They moved with practiced stealth, slipping through the shadows like wraiths, avoiding open spaces where they might be seen.

Just as they neared the edge of town, a shout broke the silence. Santiago's pulse quickened as he glanced back, catching sight of several men running toward them, their expressions tense with suspicion.

"After them!" one of the villagers shouted, his voice cutting through the quiet night. "Don't let them escape!"

The Guard broke into a silent sprint, their feet pounding against the ground as they raced through the narrow paths leading out of the village. The darkness was their ally, concealing their movements as they darted between trees and dodged low-hanging branches. Emmanuel led Isabela and Marco slightly off to one side, ensuring the group stayed spread out to avoid being an easy target.

Behind them, the sound of pursuit grew louder—the thud of hurried footsteps, the rustle of leaves, and the murmur of voices as the villagers closed in.

Santiago led the team deeper into the forest, his mind racing as he calculated their next move. They couldn't afford to be caught, not with the information they carried. The Zealots of Veritas' influence was too strong in these lands, and the reformist sympathizers had every reason to turn them over to the sect's agents if they were caught.

As they reached a dense thicket, Santiago signaled for the group to stop, crouching low behind the cover of a large tree. He motioned for silence, his finger pressed to his lips as he listened to the approaching voices. The villagers were close, but they hadn't yet pinpointed their exact location.

"We'll need to split up," Santiago whispered, his voice barely a breath. "If we stay together, we're more likely to be seen. Isabela, you and Marco head north. Rafael, you come with me to the west. Emmanuel, loop around south and intercept us by the old stone bridge."

Emmanuel gave a firm nod, his gaze resolute. "I'll draw their attention toward the southern side, keep them focused away from you."

They nodded, their expressions resolute as they prepared to part. Without another word, Isabela and Marco slipped into the shadows, moving silently through the underbrush, while

Santiago and Rafael took the opposite direction, and Emmanuel veered southward.

As he moved, Emmanuel heard the sound of footsteps drawing closer from behind. He quickened his pace, slipping through the trees with practiced stealth, occasionally pausing to break a branch or disturb the leaves, drawing the attention of their pursuers further south, away from the rest of the team.

In the thick of the forest, Emmanuel caught a glimpse of movement to his right—a villager creeping toward his direction. Emmanuel drew his dagger, crouching low as he waited for the man to come closer. In a single swift motion, he stepped forward, subduing the man silently, leaving him unconscious in the cover of the bushes.

After several tense minutes, he reached the stone bridge where he was to meet the others. Soon, Isabela and Marco emerged from the northern path, their eyes scanning the area. Moments later, Santiago and Rafael joined them, all of them visibly relieved to be reunited.

"We've put enough distance between us and the village," Santiago said, his voice low. "But we can't stay here. They'll eventually find the trail."

Emmanuel looked over his comrades, a spark of determination in his gaze. "Then let's keep moving. We can lose them completely in the forest if we stay vigilant."

The Guard moved back into the cover of the trees, their steps swift and silent as they navigated the winding paths of the forest. Emmanuel kept a steady pace, his senses alert for any signs of pursuit, his presence a quiet reassurance to the others as they delved deeper into the night.

The journey ahead would be treacherous, but together, they were prepared for whatever lay in wait, their bond unbroken and their mission resolute.

The first glimmer of dawn broke over the rugged hills as the Guard made their way through the final stretch of dense forest. The air was crisp, the stillness of the morning punctuated only by the rustle of leaves underfoot. They had traveled through the night, putting as much distance as possible between themselves and the village that had nearly exposed them.

As the forest began to thin, Santiago raised a hand, signaling the others to stop. Before them lay the remnants of an ancient monastery, half-hidden in the mist that clung to the hillsides. The structure, partially overgrown with ivy and moss, seemed almost to emerge from the earth itself, its weathered stone walls blending seamlessly with the rocky terrain.

The monastery's architecture was severe yet beautiful, its pointed arches and vaulted doorways bearing the weight of centuries. High stone towers rose toward the sky, their silhouettes stark against the dim light of the morning. The place exuded an air of solemnity, as though it held within its walls secrets too heavy for the world outside.

Santiago's gaze swept over the building, noting the details—cracks in the stone, patches of moss obscuring old engravings, and the faint remains of carvings that hinted at the monastery's former glory. He could feel the weight of history pressing down on him, an unspoken reminder of the lives that had once filled these halls, monks who had dedicated their existence to a purpose now shrouded in mystery.

"This is it," he murmured, his voice barely a whisper, as though speaking too loudly might disturb the quiet sanctity of the place. "The monastery where the Codex is said to be hidden."

Emmanuel came up beside him, his eyes narrowed as he surveyed the structure. "It feels like the stones themselves guard the Codex," he observed quietly. "This place was built for more than just shelter—it's a fortress for knowledge, a sanctuary against the unworthy."

Rafael nodded in agreement, his gaze fixed on the ancient structure. "It looks abandoned, but I wouldn't trust appearances. A place like this doesn't stay untouched for long—especially not with something as valuable as the Codex within its walls."

Isabela's eyes narrowed as she scanned the monastery's facade. "Brother Jakob spoke of traps, wards meant to deter those unworthy of the Codex. We'll need to proceed with caution. This place was built to protect its secrets, and it will not give them up easily."

The monastery, though silent and still, felt alive in its own way, as though it watched them with hidden eyes. Santiago could sense the tension in his team, each member alert and prepared for whatever awaited them within.

"Marco, take point," Santiago instructed, gesturing toward the arched entrance. "Move slowly, and stay alert. If there are traps, they'll be designed to catch those unfamiliar with the layout. We don't know what waits inside."

Marco nodded, his posture tense yet focused. He moved forward, his steps quiet and deliberate as he approached the entrance. The others followed in a careful formation, each of them maintaining a vigilant awareness of their surroundings. Emmanuel took up the rear, his presence a silent assurance as he cast a last glance over their path, ensuring they weren't being followed.

As they neared the monastery, the air seemed to grow colder, a chill that seeped through their cloaks and settled in their bones. The silence was absolute, the kind of stillness that suggested the monastery had been abandoned for a long time. Yet Santiago couldn't shake the feeling that they were being watched, that something within the stone walls observed their every step.

When they reached the entrance, they paused, each of them studying the worn stone archway that marked the threshold. Faint inscriptions, weathered by time, adorned the stone, their meaning obscured by centuries of erosion. Emmanuel stepped forward, his eyes tracing the markings, his expression contemplative.

"It's Latin," he murmured, his voice barely audible. "An old dialect, difficult to read. It speaks of wisdom, of knowledge as both a blessing and a burden."

"Then we should be prepared," Rafael said quietly. "If this place was meant to guard the Codex, it will not be without its defenses."

They stepped through the archway, entering the monastery's main hall. The room stretched out before them, vast and echoing, its high ceilings casting shadows that danced along the walls. Stone pillars lined the hall, each one intricately carved with symbols and figures that seemed to tell a story—a tale of faith and sacrifice, of monks who had devoted their lives to preserving knowledge that was both sacred and dangerous.

Sunlight filtered through the broken stained-glass windows, casting muted colors across the stone floor. Dust floated in the air, disturbed by their presence, creating a haze that softened the harsh lines of the ancient structure. The silence was profound, and every step they took seemed to echo, a reminder of how foreign they were in this place.

Santiago paused in the center of the hall, his gaze fixed on an altar at the far end of the room. It was simple, unadorned, yet it held a quiet power, a reminder of the faith that had once been practiced here. He approached it slowly, noting the faint marks left on the stone, as though hands had once rested there in prayer, seeking guidance and wisdom.

"This place was more than just a sanctuary," he said softly, his voice filled with reverence. "It was a stronghold of belief, a testament to the power of faith."

Isabela nodded, her gaze lingering on the walls. "And now it is a tomb for secrets. Whatever knowledge the Codex holds, it was deemed too powerful to share with the world."

Emmanuel stood beside Santiago, his eyes fixed on the ancient altar. "It's a place where only those of strong faith would tread," he said quietly, his tone laced with a sense of respect. "We're here not just to retrieve a relic but to preserve something beyond ourselves."

A faint shuffling sound echoed from one of the side corridors, drawing their attention. The Guard froze, each of them turning toward the source of the noise, their hands instinctively reaching for their weapons. The sound was subtle, barely noticeable, but in the silence of the monastery, it was enough to send a shiver down Santiago's spine.

He raised a hand, signaling for caution, and moved toward the corridor, his footsteps soft and measured. The others followed, their expressions tense, each of them prepared for whatever lay ahead. Emmanuel, at the rear, kept watch, his gaze sweeping over the shadows, alert for any sign of movement.

As they ventured deeper into the monastery, the sense of foreboding grew stronger, a palpable tension that seemed to press down on them from all sides. The air was heavy with the weight of untold stories, of lives that had been lived and lost within these walls. It was a place where time had stopped, where history lingered like a shadow, clinging to every stone.

They reached a small chamber at the end of the corridor, its walls lined with shelves filled with ancient tomes and scrolls. The room was untouched, preserved as though waiting for someone to rediscover its secrets. Santiago stepped forward, his gaze scanning the shelves, searching for any sign of the Codex.

"Be cautious," he whispered, his voice a warning. "If the Codex is here, it will be hidden well. We can't afford to be reckless."

Emmanuel moved to one of the shelves, his fingers hovering over the spines of the books. "These writings... they are a testament to the faith of those who came before. Each volume holds a piece of history, preserved for those who would seek truth."

The Guard spread out, each of them carefully examining the chamber, their movements slow and deliberate. The sense of anticipation was thick in the air, an unspoken understanding that they were on the brink of something monumental. Yet the knowledge that the Codex was close brought with it a sense of dread—a reminder that they were not the only ones searching for it.

As they searched, Santiago's thoughts turned to Brother Jakob's warning. The Codex was more than a relic; it was a test, a mirror that revealed the true nature of those who sought it. And he knew that they would need to approach it with both caution and humility, for only those who understood its purpose could hope to wield its power.

The monastery was silent, but Santiago sensed the secrets it held, the hidden truths that had been buried here long ago. He felt the weight of their mission settle over him, a reminder of the duty that bound them, the faith that guided them.

And as they continued their search, he knew that they were not just seeking a relic—they were confronting a legacy, a legacy that would test them in ways they had yet to understand.

The chamber was silent, dust motes drifting lazily through the dim light that seeped in from a narrow crack in the stone wall. The Guard moved slowly, their footsteps careful as they searched the room, every detail examined with purpose. Shelves lined the walls, filled with brittle scrolls and ancient tomes, each one an echo of a time long past.

Santiago's gaze scanned the titles written in Latin, their spines worn and faded. There were records of local histories, accounts of theological debates, and treatises on faith—all preserved here, untouched by time. Yet none of them matched the descriptions he had read of the Codex Veritas. If the Codex was hidden here, it would not be in plain sight. This monastery had been a sanctuary for secrets, and the Codex was undoubtedly concealed within its deepest layers.

Isabela paused by a high shelf, her fingers tracing a set of symbols carved into the wood. She called to Santiago, her voice soft, yet filled with a sense of discovery. "Captain, there's something unusual here."

Santiago crossed the room to join her, his eyes following her gesture to a series of carved symbols—circles, crosses, and geometric shapes that had been carefully etched into the wood. The arrangement of the symbols was deliberate, almost ritualistic, and they glowed faintly under Isabela's touch, as though imbued with hidden energy.

"These symbols," Isabela murmured, her brow furrowed in concentration. "They're similar to the markings on the entrance, but there's something different here. It's as though they form a pattern—a kind of map."

Marco joined them, his gaze keen as he examined the carvings. "Do you think they're instructions? Perhaps they're meant to guide us deeper into the monastery."

Santiago considered the possibility, his mind racing as he recalled Brother Jakob's words. The Codex was more than a text; it was a test, a challenge meant to deter those who sought it without understanding. If the symbols were indeed a map, they would need to follow it carefully to avoid the monastery's rumored traps.

He glanced at Isabela, nodding. "Let's record these symbols. If they are a map, we'll need to decipher them before we proceed. We can't risk wandering blindly."

Isabela reached into her pack, pulling out a small notebook and carefully sketching the symbols, her hand steady and precise. As she worked, Santiago moved to the other side of the room, where a large stone tablet rested against the wall, its surface covered in lines of ancient script.

The script was familiar, though written in an archaic dialect that was difficult to interpret. Santiago traced the words with his finger, his mind working to piece together their meaning. Slowly, the phrases took shape, forming a message that sent a shiver down his spine.

"Only the pure of heart shall proceed; only those who seek with humility shall find. The Codex reveals not only knowledge but the truth within the seeker's soul."

Emmanuel stepped closer, his eyes scanning the lines Santiago had read. "This place truly is a crucible for the soul," he said quietly. "They have woven faith and knowledge together, ensuring that only those worthy in spirit can attain the Codex."

Emmanuel's words resonated with Santiago, a reminder of the wisdom and purpose that guided them. This mission was as much a test of their faith as it was of their courage. He nodded, sensing the gravity of their task settling over the entire team.

"Captain," Rafael's voice called softly from across the room, breaking Santiago's concentration. Santiago turned to see Rafael kneeling beside an open book that lay on a low stone pedestal, its pages covered in illustrations and notes written in a spidery hand.

"This looks like a journal," Rafael said, his tone filled with curiosity. "It describes the history of this monastery, the scholars who lived here, and the knowledge they sought to preserve. But there's something more—a passage that mentions the Codex."

Santiago joined him, scanning the lines as Rafael pointed to a particular entry. The passage was written in Latin, detailing an account from a monk who had once guarded the Codex. The words were faded but still legible.

"The Codex Veritas, a relic of the old faith, lies hidden within the heart of this sanctuary, veiled by shadows and light. Those who seek it must pass through trials of spirit and mind, for only the worthy may hold its wisdom. Beware, for it reveals not just knowledge, but the essence of the soul."

Emmanuel's brow furrowed as he read the passage alongside them. "It is as Brother Jakob said—the Codex is not just a relic but a mirror. It will reveal truths not just of the world, but of ourselves."

Isabela looked up from her notes, her expression thoughtful. "Then we'll need to proceed with reverence and caution. Whatever lies ahead, we cannot approach it with arrogance or impatience."

Santiago nodded, a sense of purpose settling over him. He knew they were venturing into unknown territory, a place where faith and knowledge intertwined, where the lines between truth and illusion blurred. The Codex was a relic of immense power, and it would reveal its secrets only to those willing to face the depths of their own souls.

As they continued their search, Isabela's attention was drawn to a small, unassuming book tucked away on a shelf. She reached for it, her fingers brushing against the leather binding. When she opened it, she found the pages filled with a series of intricate diagrams and symbols, each one accompanied by lines of text in Latin.

"This is different," she whispered, her eyes scanning the page. "These diagrams... they look like instructions, but not for anything ordinary. It's almost as if they're meant to guide someone through a series of... rites."

Santiago moved closer, studying the diagrams over her shoulder. The images depicted various stages of a journey, each one marked by symbols that matched the carvings they had found on the shelves. The diagrams seemed to outline a path, a series of steps that would lead the seeker deeper into the heart of the monastery.

"It's a map," he said softly, realization dawning on him. "The path to the Codex. These rites... they're tests, challenges meant to prove the seeker's worthiness."

Emmanuel's expression grew solemn as he processed the information. "Then we're being guided, led through this place by those who came before us. This is no mere hiding place; it's a crucible meant to refine those who enter."

Santiago looked at his team, a sense of camaraderie and purpose filling him. They had been chosen for this mission not just for their skill, but for their faith and resolve. The journey ahead would test each of them, demanding more than they had ever given. But he knew that they were ready.

"This is our path," he said, his voice filled with quiet conviction. "We will follow it, step by step, with humility and strength. And whatever trials we face, we will overcome them together."

They each shared a nod of agreement, their expressions resolute. The monastery's secrets had begun to reveal themselves, guiding them toward the Codex and the knowledge it held. The journey would be long and arduous, filled with unseen dangers and challenges, but they were prepared.

As they prepared to leave the chamber and continue their search, Santiago took one last look at the symbols carved into the shelves, the ancient text that spoke of faith and truth. He felt a quiet reverence settle over him, a reminder that their mission was not just to retrieve a relic, but to protect a legacy—a legacy that transcended time and space, a testament to the enduring power of belief.

With a final glance at his team, Santiago led them forward, stepping into the unknown with a heart filled with both courage and humility. The path to the Codex lay ahead, shrouded in mystery and danger, but they would face it with unwavering resolve.

They moved deeper into the monastery, their footsteps echoing through the ancient stone halls, each step a testament to their faith and dedication. And as they ventured into the shadows, Santiago knew that they were not alone—the spirits of those who had guarded the Codex before them walked with them, guiding their way.

**Chapter 3: Trials of Faith**

The Guard moved silently through the dimly lit hallways of the monastery, each step echoing softly off the stone walls. The clues they had gathered from the monastery's carved symbols and ancient tomes guided them, yet a sense of mystery hung in the air. The weight of history pressed down upon them, making each step feel heavier as they ventured deeper into the monastery.

Santiago led the way, his gaze sharp, studying the monastery's architecture for any significant details. The stone walls bore inscriptions in Latin and Greek—words of faith, wisdom, and reverence that had weathered centuries. These halls had once been a haven for those seeking spiritual enlightenment, but now their purpose seemed foreboding.

"This way," Santiago whispered, nodding toward a staircase leading down into the lower levels.

The stairs descended in a spiral, leading them into the heart of the ancient building. The air grew colder with each step, and a faint, musty scent filled their lungs as they moved deeper into the shadows. They held their torches aloft, their flames casting eerie shadows against the walls, giving life to the carved faces of saints and martyrs etched into the stone.

Emmanuel, walking beside Rafael, murmured under his breath, "It's as though these walls carry the weight of souls who once walked here. A place sanctified by faith yet charged with the unknown."

Rafael nodded, sharing Emmanuel's unease. "It feels like this place is watching us, gauging our intent. The air itself seems… alive."

Isabela, further up, replied softly, "Faith can leave its mark on places like this. This wasn't just a building—it was a fortress of devotion. Its spirit lingers."

As they reached the bottom of the staircase, Santiago paused at the entrance to a large, imposing door. Carved into the stone archway, intricate symbols—circles representing eternity, flames symbolizing purity, and crosses marking faith—formed a complex design that seemed to pulse with latent energy.

"This must be it," Santiago murmured, his fingers tracing the carvings. "The entrance to the Inner Sanctum."

The others gathered around him, each sensing the solemnity of the moment. Emmanuel took a step forward, his face thoughtful as he examined the Latin inscription above the door. His voice was barely a whisper as he read aloud, "Intus ad veritatem viam, pauci valent pervenire—The path within leads to truth, but few are worthy to reach it."

Marco exhaled quietly, his hand resting on his sword. "Then we must prove ourselves worthy."

Santiago nodded, feeling a quiet determination settle over him. "This place was meant to guard the Codex Veritas, to keep it hidden from those who would misuse its power. If we are to retrieve it, we must be prepared to face whatever trials lie ahead."

He turned to the Guard, meeting each of their gazes. "The journey beyond this door will not be easy. These trials will test us in ways we cannot yet imagine. They will seek to break our faith, to shake our resolve. But remember this: we are bound not by our own desires, but by our duty to God and to the Church."

Emmanuel placed a hand over his heart, his eyes resolute. "The Codex is more than a relic. It is a testament to our beliefs, a symbol of the knowledge we are charged to protect. We will face these trials with humility and courage."

Isabela nodded, her gaze unwavering. "We protect the light of faith. If that calls for sacrifice, then we shall not falter."

Santiago felt a surge of pride. They were more than comrades; they were bound by a shared purpose, a calling that went beyond their individual lives. He raised his hand, resting it gently on the door as he offered a silent prayer.

"Lord, grant us strength and wisdom as we face the unknown. Guide our steps, and let our faith be our shield against the darkness."

With a deep breath, Santiago pushed the door open, its heavy weight yielding to reveal a narrow passage lined with flickering torches. The air was thick with the scent of incense, a reminder of the prayers that had once filled these halls. The path was dimly lit, shadows casting an eerie glow as they ventured forward, each step bringing them closer to the trials that awaited.

As they walked, Santiago's thoughts drifted to the teachings he had studied as a young man, the lessons that had shaped his understanding of faith. He recalled the words of Proverbs: *"Trust in the Lord with all your heart, and lean not on your own understanding."*

The passage twisted and turned, leading them deeper into the heart of the monastery. It felt as though they were walking into a labyrinth, a place designed to disorient and challenge those who entered. Santiago kept his focus, his mind steady as he followed the path laid out before them.

They came to a small chamber, its walls adorned with ancient tapestries depicting scenes of spiritual trials—figures kneeling in prayer, warriors standing against darkness, seekers reaching for enlightenment. Each image conveyed a message, a reminder of the journey they were about to undertake.

Rafael studied the tapestries, his gaze solemn. "These images... they tell a story. Each one shows a different trial, a test of faith."

Isabela nodded, her eyes lingering on a tapestry that depicted a figure kneeling before a blazing fire. "The fire of humility, the strength of resolve... these trials were meant to purify the spirit, to reveal the truth within the heart."

Emmanuel spoke softly, his words resonating with the group. "These images remind us of our own trials—our duty to protect, to serve. Each test represents a deeper truth we must face within ourselves."

Santiago turned to his team, his expression resolute. "This place was built to guard the Codex, but it was also built to guide those who sought it. We must proceed with caution, for every step we take is a step deeper into the unknown."

He led them forward, his hand resting on his sword as they approached the next door. It was marked with a single word in Latin: "Fides"—Faith.

He took a deep breath, feeling the weight of the word settle over him. Faith had been the foundation of his life, the guiding light that had led him through darkness and doubt. Now, it would be his strength as he faced the trials that lay beyond.

"We move forward together," Santiago said, his voice steady. "Our faith will guide us, and our unity will keep us strong. Whatever lies ahead, we face it as one."

With those words, he pushed open the door, leading them into the heart of the monastery's Inner Sanctum. The air grew colder, the shadows deepening as they crossed the threshold. Each of them felt the tension in the air, a sense of anticipation that settled over them like a shroud.

And as they stepped into the darkness, Santiago knew that the real journey was just beginning. The trials of faith awaited them, a series of tests that would reveal the strength of their beliefs, the depth of their courage, and the unbreakable bond that held them together.

They were more than warriors; they were guardians of a legacy, protectors of a truth that transcended time and space. And as they ventured deeper into the heart of the monastery, they knew that they would face whatever trials awaited them with unwavering faith.

The Guard moved cautiously down the dim corridor, each step bringing them closer to the chamber that lay ahead. The flickering torchlight cast shadows on the stone walls, adding an air of mystery to the monastery's Inner Sanctum. Santiago led the way, his face set in grim determination, his hand resting lightly on the hilt of his sword.

As they approached a set of intricately carved doors, Santiago felt a subtle change in the atmosphere. The air grew heavier, and there was a faint scent of incense mixed with something richer, almost intoxicating. He glanced back at the others, their faces reflecting his own tension and anticipation.

Rafael, ever watchful, raised an eyebrow. "Do you feel that, Captain? It's as if we're being… drawn in."

Santiago nodded. "Yes. This place is designed to test us, to tempt us in ways we may not expect. We need to stay focused. Whatever we find in this chamber, remember our purpose and our vow."

With a deep breath, Santiago pushed open the heavy doors, revealing a vast room filled with treasures and artifacts. The chamber was magnificent, its walls lined with gilded statues, shelves of jewels, ancient manuscripts, and paintings that glowed under the torchlight. In the center of the room, atop a raised platform, sat a large golden chalice, encrusted with precious stones that sparkled in the dim light.

The Guard stopped, momentarily stunned by the opulence surrounding them. It was as if they had stepped into a different world, a place filled with the relics of empires long gone, each item carrying its own story of wealth and power. The room was a testament to humanity's endless pursuit of glory, a collection of treasures meant to ensnare the hearts of those who sought them.

Marco took a hesitant step forward, his eyes wide as he took in the scene. "All this… here? Hidden away for centuries?"

Isabela shook her head, her voice barely a whisper. "It's magnificent, but there's something unsettling about it. This isn't a reward; it's a test."

Santiago turned to his team, his expression firm. "Isabela is right. This is the Trial of Humility. These treasures are meant to distract us, to tempt us with wealth and power. But remember our purpose here. We are not here to claim riches; we are here to retrieve the Codex, to serve a purpose greater than ourselves."

Emmanuel nodded thoughtfully, his gaze fixed on an old, intricately woven tapestry depicting a battle. "Pride can be a subtle lure, even when it's draped in noble intentions," he said quietly. "Our calling demands more than strength—it demands humility."

Santiago caught Emmanuel's eye, a silent acknowledgment passing between them. Emmanuel had always carried a quiet wisdom, a perspective shaped by his deep faith and years of service. His words echoed what they all knew but needed to remember at that moment.

Rafael, however, found his gaze lingering on a beautifully crafted sword displayed on one of the shelves. The hilt was encrusted with emeralds, and the blade glinted with an almost ethereal light. It was the kind of weapon that any warrior would covet, a symbol of status and strength.

Noticing Rafael's gaze, Santiago stepped closer, his tone quiet but firm. "Remember, my friend, Proverbs warns us of the dangers of pride and greed. 'Better to be lowly in spirit along with the oppressed than to share plunder with the proud.' Our strength is not in these earthly treasures, but in our faith and unity."

Rafael looked away from the sword, nodding. "You're right, Captain. This place is meant to test us, to see if we are worthy of the Codex."

They moved deeper into the chamber, maneuvering through the aisles of artifacts and relics. The allure of the treasures was powerful, each item whispering promises of glory, wealth, and influence. The room seemed almost alive, as if it were watching them, waiting for one of them to falter.

Isabela paused beside an ancient manuscript bound in fine leather, its pages filled with intricate illustrations and illuminated text. She felt a pull toward it, a desire to open it, to study its secrets. But she resisted, reminding herself of the purpose that had brought them here.

"This knowledge… it's meant to draw us in, to distract us from our true mission," she murmured, her fingers brushing against the edge of the manuscript before she pulled her hand away. "The Codex is more than just knowledge. It is a test of the soul."

Emmanuel stepped beside her, offering a quiet but reassuring presence. "Wisdom is a gift, but it is also a responsibility," he said, his voice calm. "True knowledge serves a higher purpose. Anything that tempts us away from that purpose is an illusion."

Santiago nodded at Emmanuel's words, his respect for his comrade's insight clear. "You're right, Emmanuel. We must keep our eyes on the path ahead. The Codex will not reveal itself to those who seek it for personal gain."

They continued through the chamber, feeling the weight of the temptation around them. The treasures were designed to appeal to their deepest desires—strength, knowledge, power—but the Guard knew these were distractions, obstacles meant to test their commitment to the mission.

As they neared the raised platform with the golden chalice, Santiago felt a shift in the air. The chalice seemed to radiate an almost magnetic energy, a pull that urged him to reach out and claim it. He could feel its allure, a promise of power and authority that whispered to his pride, tempting him with visions of glory and control.

But Santiago resisted, grounding himself in the words of Proverbs that had guided him through his life. "Pride goes before destruction, a haughty spirit before a fall." He knew that to give in to such temptation would be to fail the very purpose of his calling, to lose sight of the mission entrusted to him by the Church.

He turned to the others, his voice firm. "We must leave this place. These treasures are meant to test our resolve, to see if we can resist the lure of earthly rewards. Our mission is greater than these temptations. Let us prove our worth by walking away, by showing that our faith is stronger than any treasure."

Marco hesitated, glancing at a silver chalice set with rubies, its surface polished to a mirror-like sheen. "But Captain... these relics, this wealth. Couldn't we use it to support the Church, to strengthen our cause?"

Emmanuel placed a hand on Marco's shoulder, his voice steady. "The strength of our cause isn't measured in gold or jewels, Marco. It's measured in faith, in our commitment to what we serve. Anything less would betray our purpose."

One by one, they turned their backs on the treasures, their resolve unshaken. The room seemed to pulse with a quiet energy, acknowledging their choice to forgo the temptations laid before them. The air grew lighter, the oppressive weight of the chamber lifting as they moved toward the far exit.

As they reached the door, Santiago turned back one last time, his gaze sweeping over the treasures within the chamber. He felt a sense of peace, a quiet strength that came from knowing he and his team had passed the first test. They had chosen humility over pride, faith over greed, and unity over division.

He spoke softly, quoting a final verse from Proverbs. "Humility is the fear of the Lord; its wages are riches and honor and life." These words were a reminder of the true reward they sought, a reward that could not be measured in earthly treasures.

The Guard left the chamber, stepping through the doorway and into the next passage. The path ahead was still shrouded in mystery, the trials yet to come unknown. But they carried with them a renewed sense of purpose, a reminder of the vow that had brought them here.

As they ventured deeper into the monastery, Santiago felt a quiet assurance settle over him. They had proven their worth in the Trial of Humility, resisting the allure of power and wealth, and now they were one step closer to the Codex. The journey would not be easy, but he knew they would face whatever lay ahead with courage and faith.

For the Guard, humility was not a weakness; it was their strength, a testament to the principles that guided them. And as they moved forward, Santiago knew that they carried with them something far greater than any treasure—a purpose that would withstand the tests of time and temptation.

The Guard stood at the entrance of the next chamber, a vast stone hall stretching into darkness, its walls lined with torches casting dim, flickering light. Santiago surveyed the space, his gaze falling on a series of platforms, ropes, and barriers that crisscrossed the room. This was no ordinary chamber; it was an elaborate obstacle course, designed to test their physical strength, agility, and endurance.

He could sense the latent energy in the room, the silent challenge awaiting them. They would have to move quickly and skillfully, anticipating danger at every turn. Santiago glanced at his team, his expression serious.

"This is the Trial of Strength and Resilience," he said. "Everything in this chamber is meant to test our limits. Stay close, keep sharp, and remember to rely on each other. We cannot afford mistakes here."

Emmanuel, who often carried a quiet but resolute demeanor, gave a brief nod, his voice calm and steady. "These challenges, Captain, are like the trials spoken of in Proverbs: 'For the righteous falls seven times and rises again.' Strength isn't just about how we stand but how we rise."

Rafael nodded, his hand tightening on the hilt of his sword. "We've trained for this. Whatever traps lie ahead, we'll face them together."

Isabela glanced at the narrow paths and hanging ropes with determination. "We've faced worse than this. Our strength is in our unity."

With a final nod, Santiago took a steadying breath and led the Guard forward. They moved carefully, their senses heightened as they scanned their surroundings. The first challenge appeared to be a series of narrow beams suspended over a deep pit, each beam angled slightly differently, making it nearly impossible to walk in a straight line. Below, sharp stakes protruded from the ground, ready to catch anyone who fell.

Santiago tested the first beam, feeling it wobble slightly under his weight. "We'll have to move slowly here. Maintain your balance and keep focused."

Marco moved first, his agility serving him well as he shifted his weight with each step, arms extended for balance. He reached the end of the beam and looked back, nodding to the others. "It's tricky, but manageable."

One by one, the Guard crossed the beams, each of them maintaining their focus as they moved with careful precision. Santiago stayed close, his gaze flicking between his teammates to ensure everyone was safe. Isabela hesitated at one point, her foot slipping slightly, but Rafael reached out, steadying her with a firm grip.

"Thank you," she murmured, regaining her balance.

"Keep going," Rafael replied with a reassuring smile. "We've got this."

Emmanuel followed, his steps sure and deliberate. When he reached the other side, he glanced back, offering a few quiet words of encouragement. "Remember, fear steadies no hand, but faith gives light to each step."

Once they all reached the other side, they faced their next challenge: a series of ropes suspended from the ceiling, swaying gently over a gap that stretched the width of the room. There were no platforms to land on; they would have to swing across and grab the next rope without missing a beat.

Santiago studied the ropes, calculating the momentum they would need to move smoothly from one to the next. "We'll go in pairs. One of us will start the swing, and the other will follow. Rafael and Marco, you go first."

Rafael grabbed the first rope, testing its strength, and then leaped forward, swinging across the gap. As he released his hold and reached for the next rope, Marco followed close behind, catching up to him just as Rafael moved to the next rope in line. They moved in perfect synchronization, each anticipating the other's movements.

Isabela and Santiago followed next. The ropes were unsteady, and each swing required precise timing. Santiago could feel his muscles strain as he gripped tightly, his body swinging forward with each motion. He landed on the final platform alongside Rafael and Marco, his heart pounding.

Emmanuel, the last to go, offered a quiet prayer before gripping the rope. His timing was precise, each swing smooth and sure, and he soon landed beside them with a calm smile, his quiet confidence an anchor to the team.

They moved deeper into the chamber, approaching the next section of the obstacle course. This time, they faced a wall of shifting gears and rotating panels, each section moving in a complex pattern that left only brief gaps to pass through. The slightest misstep would mean being crushed between the gears or thrown back by the rotating panels.

Santiago studied the rhythm of the movements, his eyes narrowing as he calculated the timing. "We'll go through one by one. Wait for the gap, move quickly, and don't hesitate."

He moved first, darting between the panels, his timing precise as he slipped through the gears just as they shifted apart. He turned back to watch as Marco followed, his speed and reflexes allowing him to navigate the path with ease. Next came Rafael, his large frame barely fitting between the gaps, but he moved with a surprising grace, keeping his movements tight and controlled.

When it was Isabela's turn, she hesitated, her eyes tracking the shifting gears with a hint of uncertainty. Santiago called out to her, his voice calm. "Wait for the opening, then move quickly. You have the skill; trust yourself."

Emmanuel stepped forward beside her, his voice a steady whisper. "Trust in your steps, Isabela. Remember the words: 'The Lord will be your confidence.'" With a gentle nod of encouragement, he watched as she took a deep breath and moved forward, her movements sure as she passed through the gears unscathed.

"Good work," Santiago said as she reached him. "Let's keep moving."

As they pressed onward, they encountered a narrow path lined with traps—pressure plates hidden beneath loose stones, each one set to trigger a hidden arrow or blade. Santiago knew this would test their focus and reflexes; they had to spot the plates before stepping on them, avoiding each one with precision.

"Watch the ground closely," he instructed. "Every step matters here."

Rafael led the way, his keen eye spotting the first pressure plate. He carefully stepped over it, indicating a safe path for the others to follow. They moved in single file, each of them relying on the guidance of the one ahead. Marco, with his agility, took the lead whenever the path twisted, gracefully navigating around the traps with ease.

Santiago followed close behind, his focus absolute as he guided them through the maze of traps. They encountered arrows that shot from the walls, sharp blades that swung from above, and even pits concealed by fragile coverings. But their training had prepared them for such challenges, and they moved as one, each trusting the instincts and abilities of the other.

When they finally reached the end of the trapped path, the Guard paused to catch their breath, the weight of the trial settling over them. Their bodies were weary, their muscles aching, but their resolve remained unbroken.

"We're almost through," Santiago said, his voice filled with quiet pride. "You've all done well. Let's finish this."

They reached the final section of the chamber, where a towering wall stood before them, its surface covered in rough stone grips. At the top, a narrow ledge led to the exit. This was the final test of endurance—a climb that would push them to their limits.

Rafael grinned, his eyes gleaming with determination. "A climb to the finish line? Now that's more like it."

Santiago nodded, his own gaze steely. "We go together. Keep your grip firm and your pace steady. There's no rush, but we can't afford to fall."

One by one, they began the ascent, their hands finding purchase on the rough stones. Santiago's arms burned as he pulled himself upward, his muscles straining with each movement. The climb was steep, and the ledge seemed impossibly far, but he focused on the rhythm of his breath, pushing himself to keep going.

Marco, with his agility, took the lead, moving with an almost feline grace as he scaled the wall. He paused at intervals, glancing back to offer guidance, his voice steady and encouraging. Rafael, though less agile, used his strength to his advantage, his powerful frame allowing him to make each move with controlled precision.

Isabela climbed beside Santiago, her expression one of fierce determination. She slipped once, her foot missing a hold, but Santiago reached out, steadying her before she could lose her grip.

"Thank you," she said, her voice breathless.

"We're in this together," he replied. "One step at a time."

Emmanuel followed, his breathing steady, his presence calm and composed. He had the patience of a seasoned climber, each move calculated and sure, his focus unwavering. As they reached the top, he offered a few final words of encouragement. "Endurance isn't just in the body; it's in the spirit. And we are more resilient than we realize."

They had completed the Trial of Strength and Resilience, emerging from the ordeal exhausted but victorious. Santiago looked at his team, pride shining in his eyes.

"You've all proven yourselves today," he said, his voice filled with respect. "These trials were designed to break us, to test our limits. But we've shown that our strength lies not just in our skills, but in our unity."

Rafael grinned, wiping sweat from his brow. "We wouldn't have made it through without each other."

Marco nodded in agreement. "Every step, every move—it was a team effort."

Isabela smiled, her gaze soft. "We are more than just a Guard. We're family."

Emmanuel, standing quietly beside them, nodded in agreement. "Faith, loyalty, unity—that is what carries us through every trial. And today, we have shown that nothing can break the strength we share."

Santiago felt a surge of gratitude as he looked at each of them. They had faced the trials together, their bond unbreakable, their loyalty unwavering. He knew that no matter what challenges lay ahead, they would face them as one.

Rising to his feet, Santiago extended a hand to Isabela, helping her up. "Let's keep going. We still have a mission to complete."

Together, they stepped forward, leaving the Trial of Strength and Resilience behind, their spirits strengthened by the challenges they had overcome. They were more than warriors; they were guardians, bound by a purpose that transcended any physical test.

And as they moved toward the next chamber, Santiago knew that they carried within them a resilience that no trial could shatter—a resilience forged in faith, loyalty, and the unbreakable bond of the Iberian Guard.

The Guard entered a small, dimly lit chamber, its silence unsettling after the echoing halls and daunting obstacles they had faced. This room was different—quiet and empty, save for a soft light that seemed to emanate from nowhere, illuminating the chamber with an ethereal glow. The air was still, thick with an inexplicable weight, as if something unseen was lurking in the shadows.

Santiago took a careful step forward, his senses alert. "Stay close," he murmured. "This place doesn't feel... ordinary."

They stood in a loose circle, each of them instinctively scanning the room, searching for traps or signs of danger. But there was nothing—not a sound, not a movement, only the strange, suffocating silence.

Suddenly, the light began to shift, casting long shadows on the walls that twisted and coalesced into vaguely familiar forms. One by one, the shapes took on clarity, becoming figures they recognized from their pasts. The shadows solidified, revealing faces they had not seen in years—faces they had long since buried in memory.

Isabela was the first to react. Her eyes widened as she took in the figure before her—a woman with soft, warm eyes, her face framed by gentle curls. It was her mother, who had passed away when Isabela was still a child. The woman's expression was one of sadness, her gaze steady and piercing.

"Isabela," the figure said softly, her voice echoing in the stillness. "You left us. You left me. How could you turn your back on your family for this life?"

Isabela's breath hitched, her hand instinctively reaching for the hilt of her dagger. "You... you're not real. My mother passed long ago," she whispered, though her voice trembled.

"Your loyalty is to strangers, to men who command you. But where was your loyalty when I needed you?" the figure accused, her tone laced with sorrow.

Isabela clenched her fists, fighting the guilt that bubbled to the surface. She had always carried a sense of loss, a feeling that she had abandoned her family to pursue a life of service. But she steadied herself, recalling the words of Santiago, the wisdom he had shared with them. "'The Lord is my shepherd; I shall not want.'" Her loyalty had not been misplaced—it was a calling, a duty that went beyond her own desires.

"No," she whispered, her voice growing stronger. "I chose this path because it was right. I have dedicated my life to protecting others, to serving a purpose beyond myself. I have not turned my back on anyone—I have honored the life you gave me."

The figure wavered, its form dissolving into shadows as Isabela held her ground, her faith unwavering. She had faced her fear, her guilt, and found strength in her conviction.

Meanwhile, Marco stood frozen, staring at a young boy who now appeared before him, his face smeared with dirt, his eyes wide and filled with fear. Marco's throat tightened as he recognized the boy—one of the children from his village, a child he had tried to protect during an attack years ago.

"You promised you would keep us safe," the boy's voice quivered, his eyes brimming with unshed tears. "But you couldn't. You let them hurt us."

Marco's hands shook, his mind flooded with memories of that night—the fire, the screams, the helplessness he had felt. He had joined the Guard hoping to atone for his failure, to prevent others from experiencing the pain he could not stop. But seeing the boy now, that old wound reopened, raw and aching.

"I…" Marco's voice cracked, his guilt weighing heavily on him. He had always wondered if his service would ever be enough to make up for the lives he could not save. But he straightened, reminding himself of his purpose. "The Lord is my strength and my shield."

He took a deep breath, meeting the boy's gaze. "I carry that night with me every day. But I am not powerless anymore. I have sworn to protect, to do whatever I can to shield others from harm. My faith and my duty are what drive me forward. I will not let that night define me."

The figure blinked, the sorrow in its eyes softening as it faded back into shadow. Marco remained, his guilt eased by the knowledge that his journey had been one of redemption, not penance.

Rafael was facing his own specter—a young woman with a stern but caring expression. She looked at him with a mixture of disappointment and sorrow, her hands folded as if in prayer. She was a fellow novice he had trained with in his youth, a woman who had chosen a simpler life of faith while he had taken up the sword.

"Rafael," she said, her voice like a whisper carried on a breeze. "You chose violence over peace, power over faith. How can you still call yourself a servant of God?"

Rafael clenched his fists, feeling the old, familiar shame rise within him. He had wrestled with this question for years, wondering if he had strayed too far from the path of faith by choosing a life of combat. But his heart was steadfast, his convictions unbroken.

"I chose to defend the innocent, to be a shield for those who cannot protect themselves," he replied, his voice steady. "There is strength in faith, but there is also strength in action. I do not fight out of pride or anger. I fight out of love, out of duty. 'The righteous are as bold as a lion.' I am not defined by my weapon, but by my purpose."

The woman's expression softened, her form dissipating like mist in the sunlight. Rafael let out a long breath, his heart lighter. He had proven to himself that his faith and his calling were one and the same, a unity of purpose that no illusion could shatter.

Emmanuel, too, faced a specter—a figure from his past, a mentor who had raised him in the faith but had questioned his decision to join the Guard. The man's face was lined with disappointment, his voice carrying a mixture of sorrow and sternness.

"Emmanuel," he said, his tone heavy with reproach. "You were meant to serve in the Church, to be a shepherd of souls. Instead, you took up arms. How can you say this is God's will?"

Emmanuel looked into the eyes of his old mentor, feeling the weight of the question that had haunted him for years. But he was no longer conflicted; his path had become clear. He replied softly, his voice filled with conviction. "For everything, there is a season—a time to plant and a time to uproot, a time to build and a time to tear down. I serve the same faith, but in a way that protects those who cannot protect themselves."

His gaze held steady as he continued. "My heart remains devoted to God, and my hands to His work. I am not divided in my loyalty—I am a defender of faith, just as you taught me. And though my way may be different, I walk it with reverence."

The mentor's figure softened, the sternness fading from his expression, replaced by a look of understanding. He vanished into the shadows, leaving Emmanuel standing tall, his faith unshaken.

Santiago had been silently watching his team confront their pasts, his heart swelling with pride as each of them held firm to their faith. But he, too, was not immune to the chamber's power. A figure stepped forward from the shadows, a face he knew all too well—a soldier from his first mission, a man who had fallen under his command.

"Captain," the figure said, his tone cold. "You left me to die. You promised us glory, honor. But we were nothing but sacrifices to you."

Santiago felt a pang of sorrow, the familiar guilt resurfacing. He remembered the man's death, the helplessness he had felt, the sense that he had failed those who had entrusted him with their lives. It had been a wound he carried in silence, a burden he had never truly let go of.

But he steadied himself, reminding himself of the wisdom he had gathered over the years. "For the Lord will be your confidence and will keep your foot from being snared." His heart was not driven by pride, nor by a desire for glory. His path had been one of service, of sacrifice, and he had carried it willingly, with humility.

"You're right," he said quietly. "I was young, and I made mistakes. But I have spent my life learning, growing, and dedicating myself to a purpose greater than my own. My service is not for personal gain—it is for the people, for the lives I protect. My duty is to them, and to God. And that is where my loyalty lies."

The figure looked at him for a long moment, a flicker of respect crossing his face before he dissolved into shadow. Santiago felt a wave of peace settle over him, his past no longer a weight but a part of his journey, a reminder of the lessons he had learned.

The chamber grew quiet once more, the illusions fading back into the darkness. Each member of the Guard stood in silent reflection, their hearts steadied by the trials they had just endured. The visions had challenged them, sought to undermine their faith, but they had emerged stronger, bound by a purpose that transcended their individual fears and regrets.

Santiago looked at each of them, his gaze filled with pride. "You have all shown true strength, facing your fears without wavering. Our faith is what guides us, what keeps us grounded. No illusion, no shadow can shake what is in our hearts."

Rafael nodded, his voice filled with conviction. "We carry our past with us, but it does not define us. Our faith, our duty—these are the pillars that hold us steady."

Isabela placed a hand over her heart, her gaze soft but resolute. "We are bound by our calling, by a purpose that is greater than any one of us. Together, we are stronger."

Marco smiled, the guilt he had carried now tempered by the strength he felt. "We walk this path not alone, but as one. And we face whatever lies ahead with faith and unity."

Emmanuel added, his voice calm and steadfast, "Our mission is a sacred one. The trials we face will only fortify the bond we share, a bond rooted in faith and loyalty."

They left the chamber, their spirits unbroken, their faith unwavering. The Trial of Faith had tested their resolve, but they had emerged with a deeper understanding of their purpose and a renewed commitment to their mission.

As they moved forward into the shadows, Santiago felt a quiet confidence settle over him. The path would not be easy, but he knew that they would face it with courage, faith, and the strength of their convictions.

Santiago felt a pang of sorrow, the familiar guilt resurfacing. He remembered the man's death, the helplessness he had felt, the sense that he had failed those who had entrusted him with their lives. It had been a wound he carried in silence, a burden he had never truly let go of.

But he steadied himself, reminding himself of the wisdom he had gathered over the years. *"For the Lord will be your confidence and will keep your foot from being snared."* His heart was not driven by pride, nor by a desire for glory. His path had been one of service, of sacrifice, and he had carried it willingly, with humility.

"You're right," he said quietly. "I was young, and I made mistakes. But I have spent my life learning, growing, and dedicating myself to a purpose greater than my own. My service is not for personal gain—it is for the people, for the lives I protect. My duty is to them, and to God. And that is where my loyalty lies."

The figure looked at him for a long moment, a flicker of respect crossing his face before he dissolved into shadow. Santiago felt a wave of peace settle over him, his past no longer a weight but a part of his journey, a reminder of the lessons he had learned.

The chamber grew quiet once more, the illusions fading back into the darkness. Each member of the Guard stood in silent reflection, their hearts steadied by the trials they had just endured. The visions had challenged them, sought to undermine their faith, but they had emerged stronger, bound by a purpose that transcended their individual fears and regrets.

Santiago looked at each of them, his gaze filled with pride. "You have all shown true strength, facing your fears without wavering. Our faith is what guides us, what keeps us grounded. No illusion, no shadow can shake what is in our hearts."

Rafael nodded, his voice filled with conviction. "We carry our past with us, but it does not define us. Our faith, our duty—these are the pillars that hold us steady."

Isabela placed a hand over her heart, her gaze soft but resolute. "We are bound by our calling, by a purpose that is greater than any one of us. Together, we are stronger."

Marco smiled, the guilt he had carried now tempered by the strength he felt. "We walk this path not alone, but as one. And we face whatever lies ahead with faith and unity."

They left the chamber, their spirits unbroken, their faith unwavering. The Trial of Faith had tested their resolve, but they had emerged with a deeper understanding of their purpose and a renewed commitment to their mission.

As they moved forward into the shadows, Santiago felt a quiet confidence settle over him. The path would not be easy, but he knew that they would face it with courage, faith, and the strength of their convictions.

The Guard moved with measured steps through the winding corridors, each of them acutely aware of the challenges they had overcome and the trials they had endured. The dim light of their torches flickered against the stone walls, casting elongated shadows that danced as they pressed deeper into the heart of the monastery. Every step brought them closer to their goal—and yet a new weight had settled upon them, a silent understanding that the Codex was far more than they had originally imagined.

They emerged from the labyrinth of narrow passages into a wide, vaulted hall. At the center stood an ancient altar, its presence commanding and serene, as though it had waited silently through centuries for their arrival. The altar was carved from a single massive slab of stone, its edges worn smooth by time, but its surface intricately engraved with symbols and inscriptions that shimmered faintly under the torchlight. Around it lay scattered remnants of what might have once been offerings—crumbled candles, tarnished coins, and wilted flowers, all covered in a thick layer of dust.

Santiago halted, his gaze sweeping over the altar with a mixture of reverence and caution. "This must be it," he murmured. "The place where the monks concealed the final pieces of the puzzle."

Emmanuel stepped forward, his expression solemn. "This place... it feels like a sanctum within a sanctum. As if only those deemed worthy are meant to set eyes upon this altar."

Isabela nodded, her eyes tracing the carvings on the stone. "Whatever the Codex contains, it's clear that those who guarded it feared its potential. This altar isn't simply a resting place; it's a threshold."

The Guard approached the altar cautiously, each of them feeling a sense of awe tempered by caution. The markings on the stone seemed to shift under the torchlight, revealing themselves slowly, as if reluctant to disclose their secrets to anyone unworthy.

Rafael knelt beside the altar, brushing his fingers over a particular set of symbols. "These markings... they're not just decorative. This is a language, an ancient script." He looked up at Santiago. "It might take time, but I believe I can decipher it."

Santiago nodded, giving Rafael space to work. He, too, could sense the gravity of the altar, as though it held not only knowledge but a warning, a testament to the power contained within the Codex. The other members of the Guard formed a loose circle around Rafael, their eyes scanning the walls and the surrounding shadows, remaining vigilant.

As Rafael began to decipher the script, Marco's gaze fell upon a section of the altar where an inscription appeared in Latin, far more recent than the ancient carvings. The letters had been carefully etched, standing out starkly against the older markings. "'Here lies the path to Veritas,'" Marco read aloud, his voice barely above a whisper. "'Only those who seek not power, but truth, may proceed. The light of wisdom is also a fire that can burn.'"

A chill ran through the group as Marco's words sank in. The inscription was a reminder that the Codex was not merely a relic of historical value but a powerful object that could transform or consume those who sought it. Santiago felt the words resonate deeply, and he realized that they were on the cusp of something far greater than they had anticipated.

Rafael paused in his reading, his gaze contemplative. "The Codex Veritas... Veritas, meaning 'truth.' But perhaps it's not just any truth—it's a truth that's hidden, protected, something dangerous in its clarity."

Isabela shivered, crossing her arms as if warding off a chill. "It's as if the Codex is meant to be a test in itself, a way to expose the true intentions of those who seek it."

As they absorbed the weight of these words, Emmanuel stepped closer to the altar, his eyes drawn to a different set of symbols that glowed faintly under the torchlight. He knelt, reaching out to touch a series of interlocking circles that radiated outward from a central point.

"These symbols," Emmanuel murmured, "they represent layers of understanding, of knowledge hidden within knowledge. The monks must have used this altar to guide those who were deemed worthy through a sequence of revelations."

Santiago glanced at Emmanuel, noting the depth of insight in his words. "Then this altar may hold the final clues we need to find the Codex," he said. "But we must tread carefully. Each revelation could be a step closer to understanding the Codex—or a trap meant to deter us."

Rafael continued deciphering, his finger tracing the lines as he read aloud, translating the ancient script with care. "'Within the Codex lies not only knowledge but the power to sway minds, to reveal or conceal the truths of the world. For those unworthy, it will offer only illusions; for those with humility, it will grant the wisdom to see.'"

Isabela's face grew grave. "The Codex isn't simply a book. It's something alive, a force that responds to the intentions of the seeker."

They stood in reverent silence, the implications of Rafael's words hanging heavily in the air. Santiago looked from one member of the Guard to the next, feeling the weight of their shared purpose settle over them like a mantle.

"We have been called to protect this Codex," he said softly. "But it is clear that it is not only knowledge that needs safeguarding—it's the very essence of what the Codex holds. This isn't something we can take lightly."

Emmanuel met his gaze, his expression filled with resolve. "Then we must approach it with humility, with the understanding that we may not be given all answers, only those necessary to our mission. Our faith must guide us as much as our skill."

As they spoke, Rafael finally completed his translation, his voice reverent as he read the last passage. "'Seek the light, but do not grasp it with greed. The Codex guards its truths with a fire that will consume those who approach with pride. Only those who see the path as service, not conquest, will understand its message.'"

Santiago placed a hand on Rafael's shoulder, a quiet gratitude in his gaze. "You have done well, Rafael. This inscription is more than a clue—it's a map of intent, a reminder of why we are here."

Emmanuel gestured to a small recess beneath the altar, barely visible in the dim light. "Look here," he said, kneeling beside it. "There's something hidden within."

With steady hands, Emmanuel reached into the recess, withdrawing a small, tarnished key attached to a strip of parchment. The parchment, though fragile, bore an inscription in Latin. He unfolded it carefully, holding it close to the torchlight.

"The key will unlock the way to Veritas," Emmanuel read aloud. "To the heart of the monastery, where light and shadow merge. Enter not with pride, for it shall be your undoing. Enter with reverence, and the path will be revealed."

He looked up at the others, his expression solemn. "The final clue. This key is our passage to the Codex—but it seems even the key itself is a test."

Santiago took the key, feeling the weight of the ancient metal in his palm. He could sense the history embedded in its cold surface, a symbol of the countless lives that had once sought the Codex's wisdom. With a nod, he motioned for the others to follow as they moved toward the back of the altar, where a narrow passage lay hidden in the shadows.

They walked in silence, each of them reflecting on the discoveries they had made, the trials they had passed. Their journey had been one of endurance, faith, and resilience, but Santiago knew that they were approaching the true test—the one that would define the legacy of the Iberian Guard.

At the end of the passage, they found a door, its wood thick and weathered, marked with symbols of protection and sacrifice. Santiago inserted the key into the lock, feeling a slight resistance before it turned with a soft click. The door swung open, revealing a chamber bathed in a soft, golden light.

Inside the room, at the center of a simple stone pedestal, lay a single, ancient tome bound in faded leather. The Codex Veritas. It radiated a quiet power, an aura of knowledge and mystery that seemed to pulse with a life of its own.

The Guard approached the pedestal, each of them feeling the weight of the moment. Santiago extended a hand toward the Codex, but he hesitated, sensing that even now, the Codex was watching, waiting.

Emmanuel stepped forward, placing a hand on Santiago's shoulder. "Remember what we have learned. This is not ours to wield as we see fit. The Codex is a tool, a guide, but it demands respect. It is not simply knowledge—it is a testament to the wisdom and faith of those who came before us."

Santiago nodded, lowering his hand. "You're right, Emmanuel. This is a responsibility, not a prize."

He looked at each member of the Guard, their faces etched with the same blend of awe and determination. "We are not here to claim the Codex, but to protect it. Its knowledge is not for us to use, but to safeguard for the generations that will come after."

Isabela placed her hand over her heart, her gaze steady. "We have been given a rare and sacred duty. We must approach this with humility, remembering the words we read—only those who seek truth, not power, will understand the Codex's purpose."

Marco, who had remained silent, now spoke, his voice filled with quiet conviction. "This journey has tested us, revealed our fears and our strengths. But through it all, we have stood together. Whatever lies ahead, we face it as one."

Rafael looked at the Codex, his gaze soft but resolute. "We will protect it, not just with our lives, but with our loyalty, our honor, and our faith. We are the Iberian Guard. We are bound by a purpose that goes beyond us."

Together, they knelt before the Codex, offering a silent prayer, a vow of guardianship and reverence. In that moment, they felt the weight of their mission settle upon them, a mantle of responsibility that they would carry with honor.

Rising, Santiago turned to lead them back through the monastery, the Codex now secure in its resting place, protected by those who understood its true purpose. They had found the final clues, the path to Veritas, but they had also found something greater—a renewed sense of their mission, a bond strengthened by faith and sacrifice.

As they stepped into the cool night air outside the monastery, Santiago felt a sense of peace settle over him. They had faced the trials, discovered the truth, and emerged stronger. And now, they were the guardians of a legacy that would endure, a testament to the power of faith, wisdom, and the unity of the Iberian Guard.

**Chapter 4: Shadows of Deception**

The Guard exited the monastery as the sun dipped below the horizon, casting long shadows across the landscape. They moved quickly, slipping into the cover of the nearby forest, hearts still racing from the trials within. The weight of their recent experiences hung heavily on them, yet an unspoken understanding passed between them. They had succeeded where others might have faltered, emerging with the knowledge and clues needed to safeguard the Codex.

Once they reached a small, secluded clearing, Santiago motioned for everyone to gather. They formed a circle, their faces illuminated by the fading light. Each of them bore the marks of exhaustion, yet there was a fierce determination in their eyes.

Santiago surveyed his team, his gaze steady and serious. "We've secured the knowledge, but our mission is far from over. The Codex is safe in its hidden place, but as long as the reformists are searching, it remains vulnerable. We cannot let them discover its true location."

Rafael nodded, his face thoughtful. "With each rumor that spreads, more eyes will turn to the Codex. Reformist sympathizers and agents are everywhere, ready to report anything that might lead them to it."

Emmanuel, who had been silent up to this point, crossed his arms and leaned against a nearby tree. "They've grown bolder with each passing year. If they hear whispers of the Codex being within their reach, they'll come in greater numbers, maybe even bringing their elite spies and soldiers."

Isabela looked around at her comrades, her brows furrowed with concern. "So how do we keep them away without revealing its true location? They're relentless—they won't stop until they find what they're looking for."

Santiago's gaze was intense as he considered her question. "The solution lies in misdirection. We know their network is vast but not infallible. If we feed them false information—false locations for the Codex—we can lead them astray."

Marco's eyes brightened as he began to understand Santiago's plan. "A series of decoy locations. Each one carefully placed to lure them in, wasting their time and resources."

"Exactly," Santiago confirmed. "If we spread rumors of the Codex's location in remote areas, they'll divide their forces, sending scouts and agents to these places. It'll take time and energy to confirm or disprove each rumor."

Emmanuel nodded, a calculating look crossing his face. "And we'll make sure each false trail is heavily guarded. We can take out any reformist cells that approach the decoy sites, which will also instill fear and hesitation among their ranks."

Isabela's face grew serious as she listened. "We'll need to be strategic in choosing these locations. Places isolated enough that the reformists can believe the Codex is hidden there, yet remote enough for us to operate without drawing unnecessary attention."

Santiago glanced around the circle, making eye contact with each member of the team. "Every rumor we start, every location we protect, must be meticulously planned. We'll let these rumors grow, embellishing them with details that make them sound credible. The reformists' curiosity will do the rest."

Rafael rubbed his chin thoughtfully. "We could even create local legends around these places. Stories of hidden dangers, cursed relics—anything that adds to the mystique and drives the reformists into our traps."

Marco smirked. "Imagine it. Rumors of a remote cave, its entrance sealed for centuries, or a forgotten crypt in the woods, said to guard ancient knowledge. They'll believe it; they're looking for anything to undermine the Church's hold on sacred artifacts."

Santiago nodded approvingly. "Exactly. We'll turn their obsession with finding the Codex into a game of shadows and whispers. Each false lead will have its own layer of mystery. If we do this correctly, they'll fear each location, uncertain of what they're truly pursuing."

Emmanuel spoke up again, his voice calm yet firm. "But this strategy isn't without its dangers. We'll be putting ourselves in the reformists' path, drawing their attention. If any of them survive, they'll know they're being deceived, and the Codex's true location could be in even greater jeopardy."

Santiago acknowledged Emmanuel's point with a nod. "You're right. This won't be without risk. Every time we engage with the reformists, we have to ensure that none of their agents escape. Their fear and confusion must remain intact, and their belief in these false leads must be absolute."

Isabela looked thoughtful. "We could recruit local informants, people loyal to the Church, who can spread these stories for us. That way, we avoid revealing ourselves directly, and the reformists would hear the rumors through the townsfolk."

Rafael grinned. "Not to mention, a local story holds more weight than a whispered tale from a stranger. If villagers talk of a cursed monastery in the mountains, it'll sound like genuine local folklore. It'll be harder for the reformists to doubt."

Santiago nodded, impressed by the depth of his team's understanding. "Precisely. This is why we operate as a unit, each of us contributing to a larger purpose. We'll need to move swiftly, placing these rumors in key towns and villages before the reformists can catch wind of our tactics."

Marco adjusted his grip on his sword, a confident gleam in his eyes. "And what of the reformist scouts who do come? Do we eliminate them quietly or leave some behind to spread the fear further?"

Santiago's expression hardened. "Only those who pose a direct threat to the operation will be eliminated. We don't want to raise suspicions of a coordinated attack on their side, just enough confusion to keep them guessing."

Emmanuel's gaze sharpened, his tactical mind at work. "And we can vary the way each rumor unfolds. Some locations could be patrolled by local allies, while others lie unguarded but shrouded in mystery. This will keep the reformists from identifying a pattern."

Isabela looked at Santiago, her voice resolute. "You have my loyalty and my sword, Captain. We will protect the Codex with everything we have. But do we have a backup plan in case they uncover the true location?"

Santiago's jaw set, his eyes flashing with determination. "If it comes to that, we fall back to Rome. The Pope must be informed, and we'll take whatever steps are necessary to secure the Codex, even if it means moving it once more. But our goal is to make sure it never comes to that."

He took a deep breath, feeling the gravity of the mission pressing down on him. "Remember, we are not merely protectors of a relic; we are protectors of the faith, of a history that must be safeguarded at all costs. The Codex is more than just knowledge—it's a beacon. If the reformists gain access to it, they'll twist it to fit their agenda, and countless lives could be influenced by lies."

The team fell into a momentary silence, absorbing the weight of Santiago's words. Each of them understood the gravity of their mission. The Codex's potential was vast, capable of inspiring or manipulating countless followers. If the reformists corrupted its teachings, it could sway the course of faith across the lands.

Finally, Santiago broke the silence, his voice calm but filled with purpose. "We'll begin our preparations at dawn. Tonight, we rest and take stock of our resources. Marco and Emmanuel, start charting potential decoy locations. Rafael and Isabela, prepare the supplies we'll need for the journey. I'll work on securing our contacts in nearby towns."

Each member nodded, slipping seamlessly into their roles. The camaraderie and trust between them was a silent testament to the years they had served together, their lives intertwined by duty and loyalty.

As they prepared to move forward with Santiago's plan, Emmanuel spoke, his voice carrying a note of admiration. "We may walk in shadows, Captain, but it's clear we do so to protect the light. Whatever challenges come our way, we're ready."

Santiago offered him a rare, appreciative smile. "Then let's move with purpose, my friend. We are the guardians of this legacy, and we will not let it fall."

The Guard spent the night in the forest, planning each aspect of their deception with meticulous care. The Codex's true location was safe for now, but they knew that this was only the beginning. Their journey would be long, filled with dangers and uncertainties, yet each of them felt a renewed sense of purpose.

And as dawn broke over the horizon, casting its first light across the land, the Guard set forth with a quiet determination, their hearts united by a common goal—to protect the Codex and preserve the truth, no matter the cost.

The early morning sun cast a soft glow over the landscape as Isabela and Emmanuel approached the small town of Burkhart. Nestled between rolling hills and farmland, Burkhart appeared unremarkable at first glance—just another quiet village with narrow streets, cobblestone paths, and the earthy scent of freshly tilled soil. But to the Guard, this unassuming town held strategic value. Known for harboring reformist sympathizers who harbored suspicions about the Church, Burkhart was the perfect place to sow seeds of doubt, intrigue, and a touch of fear.

Emmanuel glanced at Isabela, his eyes filled with a quiet intensity. "We need to tread carefully here," he said, his tone measured. "These villagers are wary of strangers, especially those who might look like they're prying. The wrong word could turn them against us. We'll need to be subtle."

Isabela adjusted the hood of her cloak, letting a few strands of her dark hair fall forward. "We're just pilgrims," she replied, her voice soft but resolute. "Travelers on a journey to uncover forgotten wisdom, perhaps. And if anyone asks... there might be a touch of mystery surrounding where we've been."

Emmanuel nodded approvingly. "Good. The less we say, the more they'll fill in the blanks themselves."

They entered the town at a steady, unhurried pace, adopting a relaxed manner. Townsfolk bustled about, busy with their morning routines—vendors arranged wares at their stalls, farmers carted fresh produce, and villagers exchanged gossip and news. Yet, there was a noticeable tension in the air; whispered conversations halted briefly as the two strangers approached, and curious, suspicious eyes followed their every move.

Emmanuel led them toward a modest inn near the center of the square, its sign swaying gently in the breeze. "Let's start here," he murmured. "A good place for travelers to rest and... share tales of things best left undisturbed."

Isabela offered a faint smile, catching his meaning. Together, they entered the inn, where the cozy interior smelled faintly of ale and aged wood. A handful of patrons sat at rough wooden tables, engaged in quiet conversation or an early drink.

Approaching the bar, they were greeted by a stout man with a thick beard and a stained apron. "Morning, travelers. Looking for a meal or perhaps a drink to warm you up?"

Emmanuel nodded with a casual smile. "A bit of both, actually. We've been on the road a long time, and a warm meal and ale would do us well."

The innkeeper nodded, glancing at them with curiosity. "Well, you're in the right place. Find yourselves a seat, and I'll bring something out for you shortly."

They settled at a table near the hearth, where they could observe the other patrons without drawing attention. Isabela pulled her cloak closer around her, casting her gaze over the room as if taking in the rustic charm of the place.

Emmanuel leaned forward, his voice barely a whisper. "Follow my lead," he murmured. "We'll let them overhear exactly what we want them to."

Isabela gave a slight nod, her posture relaxed but her attention focused.

After a few moments, the innkeeper returned with a pitcher of ale and two wooden mugs. He set them down, nodded, and retreated to tend to other customers. Emmanuel poured them each a drink and took a long sip, letting out a satisfied sigh loud enough for nearby patrons to hear.

"Hard to believe a place like that even exists," he said, loud enough for his voice to carry. "Hidden so far up in the mountains, kept secret for centuries... if it weren't for that old guide, I'd never have believed it."

Isabela raised an eyebrow, playing along. "I'm still not sure I do believe it," she replied skeptically. "A hidden monastery, guarded by ancient monks, filled with relics and forbidden knowledge? Sounds like a tale for children."

Nearby patrons began to take notice, their quiet conversations fading as they subtly leaned in to listen.

Emmanuel shrugged, his tone still casual. "I thought so too, but after what we saw... it's hard to deny. They say the place is protected by something... unnatural. Pietro—the guide—said he'd known people who tried to find it, only to disappear. Or worse, they returned with stories of shadows in the trees, strange voices whispering warnings. They say the monastery knows who approaches, and those with ill intentions are turned away... or never return at all."

The man at the next table glanced over, clearly interested. Emmanuel pretended not to notice, continuing as if the conversation were just between himself and Isabela.

"And it's not just the monastery itself," he went on, lowering his voice slightly. "It's the entire path up there. Pietro warned us of unnatural occurrences—a strange mist that confuses travelers, footsteps echoing behind you with no one there, glimpses of figures just beyond the treeline that vanish when you look directly at them."

Isabela took a sip of her ale, pretending to dismiss his claims even as she kept her voice low enough to create an air of secrecy. "Well, if that's true, then maybe there's a reason it's hidden. Perhaps some knowledge isn't meant to be found."

The man at the neighboring table could no longer contain his curiosity. "Pardon me, but I couldn't help overhearing," he said, glancing between Emmanuel and Isabela. "You're saying there's a hidden monastery nearby, protected by… supernatural forces?"

Emmanuel turned to him with a faint smile, as if hesitant to indulge the man's curiosity. "Just some stories we heard on the road. Could be nothing but superstition, but the guide seemed certain. He said it was somewhere up in the northern mountains, well-hidden, known only to a few. And he spoke of a powerful relic kept within—something that, according to legend, has guarded the monastery for generations."

The man's eyes widened. "And people… disappear?"

Isabela leaned forward slightly, lowering her voice to a conspiratorial whisper. "That's what he said. Anyone who approaches with intentions of power or conquest finds themselves… lost. Those who return speak of hauntings, of warnings whispered on the wind, as if the monastery itself is warding off intruders."

At this point, the innkeeper, who had been lingering nearby with interest, came over, setting down their food with a curious look. "Did I overhear you speaking of a monastery guarded by… spirits?"

Emmanuel gave a modest shrug. "Who knows? Could just be local tales. But they do say the monks took vows not only of silence but to protect the knowledge within, no matter the cost. It's said that the very land they're on is cursed to any who seek to misuse the relics hidden within."

The innkeeper frowned thoughtfully. "Sounds like the kind of place some folks around here might be interested in—those who don't exactly care for the Church's ways. Stories like that might appeal to the curious... or the rebellious."

Isabela smiled knowingly. "Well, if there's something worth finding out there, I'm sure certain people will be drawn to it, for better or worse."

With that, they returned to their meal, speaking in lower voices now but aware that their whispered hints had already piqued the interest of the other patrons. By the time they left the inn, they could hear the beginnings of excited conversations, hushed whispers that would soon spread throughout the town.

Outside, Isabela gave Emmanuel a satisfied nod. "That should get them talking," she murmured. "Now we just need to keep a low profile and let them spin the tale for us."

Emmanuel nodded, his gaze scanning the village square. "Let's head to the market. We'll mention it here and there, just enough to fuel the fire, then leave them to speculate."

They separated, weaving through the crowd, each dropping subtle hints at different stalls. Emmanuel picked up a small carved cross from a vendor, inspecting it thoughtfully as he spoke loud enough for nearby shoppers to hear. "Reminds me of that place Pietro showed us. Strange carvings on every wall, things I've never seen anywhere else. He said they held power... and that we were fortunate to leave unharmed."

A few villagers nearby exchanged glances, their interest piqued by his cryptic remark.

Meanwhile, Isabela drifted near a textile stall, admiring a length of fabric as she murmured to the vendor, "The guide told us it was a place only the pure-hearted could leave. They say even the light seems darker there, and shadows move where none should be."

The vendor looked up, intrigued. "You saw such a place?"

Isabela shrugged, her expression noncommittal. "Who can say? But if someone's determined enough to find it, they may learn that some secrets aren't meant to be unearthed."

As the sun dipped lower in the sky, Emmanuel and Isabela regrouped at the town's edge, watching as the seeds they had sown took root among the villagers. The whispers of a hidden, haunted monastery, guarded by unseen forces, had already started to spread.

Emmanuel looked toward the mountains, a slight smile on his face. "The reformist sympathizers will hear of this soon enough, and they'll send people to investigate. Let them."

Isabela nodded. "And when they do, they'll find only shadows… or perhaps something worse if they're not careful."

They left Burkhart quietly, confident that the rumors would continue to grow in their absence. At their camp, Santiago was waiting, his expression one of anticipation as they recounted their success.

"Perfect," Santiago said, his tone filled with satisfaction. "We'll monitor the area from a distance and ensure the legend grows. The more tales of curses and hauntings, the less likely they are to get close to the truth."

As they prepared for the next phase of their mission, Emmanuel and Isabela shared a look of quiet satisfaction. They were not only guardians of the Codex but also masters of deception, protectors of a legend that would shield the Codex from those who sought it for power. And as they looked back toward Burkhart, they knew that the whispers of curses and shadows would only grow, creating a mystery that might deter even the boldest seekers.

As the dense forest settled into the hush of dusk, Rafael and Marco crouched in the undergrowth along a narrow trail winding toward the rumored location of the Codex. This decoy, carefully planted by Isabela and Emmanuel, had successfully lured a reformist scout party toward the supposed hidden monastery. Now, the Guard lay in wait, turning the forest into an unseen battlefield, ready to ensnare their enemies within the dense maze of shadows and mist.

Rafael adjusted his position, silently checking his weapons. Every movement was practiced and soundless. Marco lay a few feet to his left, his figure camouflaged against the dark green and brown of the forest floor. Both were seasoned warriors, sharing an unspoken understanding, each attuned to the faintest sound, the slightest shift in the air. Tonight, they would become the nightmare lurking in the shadows, the guardians of a path that led to nowhere but death.

The two exchanged a brief nod as the forest thickened with mist, casting an eerie atmosphere around them. Shadows stretched and shifted, and the growing haze veiled the path with an unsettling gray shroud, giving their ambush an almost supernatural edge. Rafael took a deep breath, letting the silence of the forest settle over him as he blended into the surroundings, becoming nothing more than a whisper of danger waiting to strike.

Suddenly, Marco's voice, barely more than a breath, reached Rafael's ear. "Two figures, coming up the ridge. Slow pace. They're cautious."

Rafael nodded. "They know the risk of seeking something like the Codex," he murmured. "Let's make sure they don't return to tell of it."

The two reformist scouts moved cautiously along the path, their faces tense as they peered through the mist, the silence pressing in on them. Their eyes flickered toward each shadow, their steps tentative, as though sensing the unseen eyes watching them from the dark. Rafael noted their drawn weapons, the way their hands hovered, and the tension in their bodies. They were alert, expecting trouble. Yet even the most prepared couldn't escape what they couldn't see.

Rafael gave a subtle nod, signaling Marco to move. The two Guard members shifted like shadows themselves, flowing silently into position. Just as the scouts reached a bend in the path, Rafael and Marco struck.

In an instant, Marco's dagger found the throat of the lead scout. The man had only a second to widen his eyes in alarm before he slumped to the ground, Marco's hand pressing firmly over his mouth to muffle any sound. Meanwhile, Rafael's blade flashed toward the second scout, catching him by surprise. The sword sliced cleanly across his neck, sending him sprawling into the underbrush, blood pooling beneath him as he lay still.

In the quiet aftermath, Rafael and Marco quickly pulled the bodies into the foliage, erasing any trace of the ambush. They worked with calculated precision, knowing that the absence of obvious clues would sow fear among those who found the scene later. The forest would seem haunted, the path a cursed trail where comrades vanished without a trace.

"Efficient," Marco murmured, his eyes gleaming with satisfaction as he wiped his blade clean.

Rafael nodded, his expression dark with purpose. "It's only the beginning. Let's make sure they never feel safe, even in the open."

After concealing the bodies, the two retreated to another vantage point further up the path, ready to intercept any other reformists who might venture near.

The hours passed in tense silence. As the moon rose, casting a faint silver glow over the mist, Rafael and Marco heard the distinct crunch of footsteps approaching—a larger group this time. Rafael narrowed his eyes, counting four figures moving cautiously through the dense mist. They were visibly wary, each step slow and deliberate as they scanned the shadows around them. News of their missing scouts must have reached them, stirring unease and heightening their sense of danger. But their caution wouldn't save them from what they couldn't see.

Rafael exchanged a brief look with Marco. This was the moment to instill true fear. With a nod, he signaled Marco to wait as he picked up a small stone and tossed it into the brush off the trail. The soft rustle drew the reformists' attention, their heads snapping in the direction of the sound, weapons at the ready.

The shadows shifted, and in their moment of distraction, Rafael and Marco moved, emerging from the mist like wraiths. Rafael struck first, his sword piercing through the ribs of the nearest man, muffling his gasp with a hand over his mouth. Marco followed, his dagger finding the neck of the second man, who barely had a moment to register the attack before he crumpled to the ground.

The remaining two scouts spun around, panic seizing them as they glimpsed shapes flickering in and out of the mist, figures they couldn't pinpoint. Heartbeats hammered in the heavy silence as Rafael and Marco faded back into the shadows, making it seem as though the darkness itself had swallowed the fallen men.

One of the reformists, his face pale with fear, started to back away, his gaze darting around as if he expected another shadow to strike at any moment. "We... we need to get out of here," he stammered, his voice quivering.

His companion, equally unnerved, nodded, gripping his sword with shaking hands. But before they could retreat, Rafael moved again, stepping from the shadows and striking one of the men with deadly precision. Marco followed close behind, dispatching the other scout swiftly, leaving no sound save for the faint rustle of the leaves as their bodies slumped to the forest floor.

But this time, they allowed one scout, an inexperienced youth with terror in his eyes, to slip from their grasp. As he stumbled back down the trail, his breath ragged and his eyes darting frantically, he was unaware that the Guard allowed him to flee. From his perspective, the shadows themselves seemed to be alive, watching, stalking. The faint sounds of footsteps echoed around him, and he could feel an ominous presence lingering at every turn.

As the youth reached the edge of the forest, he didn't look back. In his mind, he was certain he'd escaped a haunted forest, one filled with malevolent spirits guarding a cursed monastery. His comrades had been taken by something otherworldly, something that lurked just beyond sight.

Marco watched him disappear, a grim smile on his face. "He'll carry the story back to the others. By tomorrow, they'll think this entire path is haunted."

"Let them believe it," Rafael replied, his voice dark with satisfaction. "Fear will do more damage to their morale than any ambush. They'll be expecting a curse around every corner."

The two Guard members resumed their positions, content to let the rumor spread among their enemies. They knew the reformists would tread carefully now, each new arrival weighed down by the stories of those who had vanished on the cursed trail.

The hours slipped by, but dawn brought another pair of reformist scouts, moving even more cautiously than their predecessors. The young men's eyes flitted toward every rustle in the leaves, and every snap of a twig sent them spinning around, gripping their weapons tighter.

Rafael and Marco waited, allowing the scouts to walk deeper into the mist-covered trail before closing in. As the first scout stepped into a patch of shadow, Rafael moved like a phantom, his blade flashing through the air and striking the man across the chest. Blood spilled as the man stumbled, his eyes wide with horror.

Marco, swift and silent, dispatched the second scout with a well-aimed throw of his dagger. The scout dropped without a sound, his body slumping into the underbrush.

As the morning light filtered through the mist, casting long shadows over the scene, the eerie silence seemed to grow, enveloping the forest like a shroud. Rafael glanced back at the concealed bodies, his face grim.

"Let the reformists believe the Codex lies here, guarded by forces beyond their understanding," he said quietly. "With each scout that disappears, this place will gain a reputation—a cursed, haunted trail where none return."

Marco's gaze darkened with conviction. "We've planted the seeds of fear. Soon, they won't dare tread this path, and their ranks will thin with each failed attempt. The whispers we've started will take on a life of their own."

With their mission accomplished, they moved stealthily through the trees to their meeting point, where Santiago and the others awaited. As they emerged from the shadows, Santiago offered a nod of approval, his expression filled with quiet pride.

Emmanuel listened intently as Rafael and Marco recounted the events, a look of satisfaction crossing his face. "A cursed path," he murmured, "guarded by shadows and silent sentinels. Let them come, but let them come afraid. They'll know they face more than mere men."

Isabela crossed her arms, a faint smile tugging at her lips. "By the time the next group arrives, they'll be so consumed by fear they won't know what's real and what's imagined. We've created a myth, and it will be as powerful a defense as any weapon."

The Guard exchanged determined glances, their resolve unwavering. They had not only defended the Codex but had also woven a story that would serve as a warning to any who dared follow.

"Did everything go according to plan?" Santiago asked.

Rafael nodded, his expression somber but satisfied. "They won't be coming back. And the trail we left will serve as a warning to any others who dare follow."

Isabela crossed her arms, her gaze thoughtful. "Good. The reformists will begin to understand that the Codex is more than just a relic—it's a force beyond their reach. Each of their losses strengthens the legend, and soon they'll hesitate to send more."

Santiago looked over his team, pride evident in his eyes. "We are creating something they cannot fight with weapons alone—a reputation, a story of danger and mystery. With every rumor and every ambush, we reinforce the myth of the Codex as an untouchable relic."

Emmanuel nodded, his voice steady. "We're not just guarding the Codex; we're guarding the faith it represents. Every reformist cell we dismantle, every rumor we spread—it all strengthens our cause."

They each felt a renewed sense of purpose, a commitment that went beyond physical battle. They were crafting a legacy, a shield of fear and mystery that would protect the Codex long after they were gone. The path to the Codex would become more than a mere trail—it would become a legend of peril and death, a place where seekers of forbidden knowledge met an untimely end.

As they prepared to leave, Santiago cast one last look back at the path, the forest now eerily silent, shadows playing along the twisted branches like silent sentinels. The air held an almost sacred stillness, a quiet reverence marking the trail that had claimed the lives of those who sought power they were never meant to hold. Santiago knew that they had laid the foundation of something far greater than a mere warning; they had kindled the beginnings of a legend, one that would spread through whispers, fueled by fear and uncertainty.

Turning back to his team, Santiago's gaze was resolute, his voice steady. "We've done well here, but this is only the beginning. The Codex's safety depends on our ability to mislead, to make them doubt every step they take."

Isabela met his eyes, a flicker of pride and determination in her expression. "We've given them something they'll struggle to counter—a story they can't fight. And the more they fail, the more they'll question if they can ever find the Codex."

"Exactly," Rafael added. "Fear is as much a weapon as any blade, and we'll wield it to keep the Codex safe."

Emmanuel spoke, his tone reflective but firm. "Every reformist who disappears or fails adds to the Codex's myth. Soon, they'll find themselves haunted by the idea of the Codex more than the Codex itself."

Santiago nodded, glancing over his team with a sense of gratitude and admiration. "Then let's continue. We'll set more trails, lay more traps, and feed them all the false leads they can handle. Every false lead buys us time, and every step we take solidifies the Codex's true legacy."

With that, the Guard moved away from the ambush site, leaving behind an eerie, silent path that held no trace of their presence—only the bodies of those who had dared to seek what was forbidden. The forest seemed to close around the trail, swallowing it whole, as if hiding the secret once again.

Together, the Guard slipped into the shadows, blending seamlessly into the wilderness, their minds already turning toward the next decoy, the next set of whispers to sow, the next myth to create. For as long as they breathed, they would protect the Codex and the faith it symbolized—not only with their skill and might but with the legend they had begun to weave.

They had become more than just protectors; they were architects of myth, guardians of an enduring mystery that would keep the Codex hidden, forever out of reach of those who sought to exploit its power. And as they moved onward, their hearts were filled with a solemn conviction, knowing that their mission was not merely to guard but to shape history, one whisper, one false trail, and one fallen reformist at a time.

The Guard moved through the dimly lit streets of a nearby village, their hoods pulled low and their steps quiet. As they passed clusters of villagers huddled by the fires, the conversations paused, eyes narrowing as they noticed the strangers' arrival. Santiago exchanged a brief nod with Isabela, signaling her to begin. This was a different kind of weapon they were wielding—fear sharpened by whispers and mystery.

Isabela and Emmanuel settled near a gathering of locals in the small tavern, the murmur of their conversation blending with the patrons' voices. They exchanged quiet glances, allowing their whispers to drift just loud enough to be overheard by curious ears.

"Did you hear?" Isabela murmured, her voice carrying a tremor. "Another party set out to find the ancient relic, but none of them returned. The forest took them."

Emmanuel leaned in, his voice lower, laced with a quiet urgency. "They say the Codex protects itself. That those who seek it for power will never find their way back. Some say they vanished without a trace; others whisper that the shadows themselves swallowed them whole."

A nearby villager, an older man with a weathered face, cast a sidelong glance at Emmanuel. "What do you mean... vanished?" he asked cautiously, his voice barely above a whisper.

Emmanuel's gaze was distant, his expression haunted. "Only God knows. They went into the woods seeking answers, but it seems the Codex has a mind of its own—a will to protect itself from those who would misuse it. They say those who have no true faith are cursed to wander forever."

A hush fell over the room, a tension palpable in the air as the villagers exchanged uneasy glances. One woman crossed herself, muttering a prayer under her breath, while others listened in silence, their expressions growing grim.

A younger man at the edge of the group, who had been listening intently, finally spoke up, his tone skeptical yet tinged with fear. "You're saying a book has... power? Enough to consume men?"

Isabela nodded solemnly, her gaze meeting his with an intensity that left little room for doubt. "The Codex is not just any book. It was written by hands guided by something beyond our understanding. It's said to hold truths that could shake the very foundations of our beliefs. Perhaps... it doesn't want to be found."

The conversation drifted back into whispers, the tale already morphing in the villagers' minds. As Emmanuel and Isabela subtly withdrew, Santiago observed the effect their words had left. Whispers spread, each villager sharing what they had overheard, with each retelling growing in detail and menace.

As they stepped out of the tavern, Isabela cast a quick glance back. She could already see the beginnings of a rumor taking root, one that would spread like wildfire. "We've planted the seed," she murmured. "Now let's see how fear shapes it."

The next day, word began spreading across the town and into surrounding villages. Stories emerged of travelers disappearing, of shadows moving through the woods, and of strange sounds echoing from within the trees at night. The Guard was deliberate in allowing the legend to grow, nudging it in the right direction whenever they encountered an opportunity.

Rafael and Marco took to the outskirts, subtly encouraging locals to speak of the Codex with reverence and caution. They added hints of danger to the tale, speaking of a "guardianship of spirits," or a "curse upon those who dare to seek knowledge forbidden by the Church."

At one point, a farmer's wife approached Rafael, her voice filled with curiosity and fear. "We've heard that the Codex is hidden somewhere in the old monastery, but that those who try to find it never come back. My husband says it's nonsense, but... people say you can hear voices calling from the trees at night."

Rafael feigned solemnity, casting a careful look over his shoulder as if wary of unseen eyes. "The Codex is not meant to be found by just anyone," he replied, his voice a low murmur. "It protects itself... or rather, something protects it. No one who goes looking with greed in their heart returns whole, if at all."

The woman shivered, her hand rising instinctively to clutch at the cross around her neck. "Then... it's cursed?"

He nodded gravely, allowing the pause to linger. "The curse is not to frighten, but to warn. It seeks only those worthy. Perhaps it's best left as it is—a mystery beyond us all."

By the end of the week, the fear had taken on a life of its own. Parents told their children to avoid the forests, lest the "Codex spirits" claim them. Farmers avoided the woods after sunset, and some spoke of seeing strange lights flickering among the trees at night. The rumor had grown into a myth, reshaped by each retelling, filling the villages with an unease that kept curious souls at bay.

As word spread, the reformists began to hear of the Codex's supposed resting place. Santiago had expected as much; no doubt they would be curious enough to send scouts again, but this time the legend would reach them first, instilling caution and perhaps even fear.

The reformists' whispers were edged with suspicion and wariness. Tales of failed search parties grew with each passing day—stories of mysterious voices, of paths that seemed to twist and lead nowhere, of men returning with a haunted look, speaking of "watchful eyes in the shadows."

The Guard observed with satisfaction, knowing that they had achieved the first step in their mission. The Codex had become something beyond a mere artifact; it was now a story, a myth that the reformists could not easily unravel. Each whisper, each new layer of fear, solidified the idea that the Codex was protected not just by men, but by something far greater.

Back at their temporary base, the Guard gathered, their expressions serious but tinged with satisfaction. Santiago looked at his team, pride evident in his eyes.

"You've all done well," he said. "The Codex is now more than a secret—it's a legend. We've planted enough fear to deter all but the most determined from seeking it."

Emmanuel spoke up, his tone reflective. "Legends have power. The more they hear of vanished search parties and spirits guarding the Codex, the less they'll question its secrecy. In time, they may fear it more than they desire it."

Rafael nodded. "Fear is a stronger deterrent than any wall or lock. Let them believe that the Codex watches those who seek it, that it punishes greed and rewards humility. Soon, even the reformists will wonder if it's worth the risk."

Santiago's gaze sharpened, a glint of determination in his eyes. "Our work is not over. We must keep the legend alive, reinforce it in any way we can. As long as the Codex remains a source of mystery and dread, it will stay protected."

They all nodded, a renewed sense of purpose settling over them. They had become the architects of a legend, the guardians of a myth that would shield the Codex more effectively than any blade or fortress.

As they moved forward, each of them knew the path would be fraught with dangers and sacrifices. But the mission was clear, and their resolve was unbreakable. The Codex would remain safe, a relic shrouded in legend, its secrets hidden from those unworthy of its power.

And as the villagers continued to spread tales of haunted woods and cursed relics, the Guard faded back into the shadows, unseen yet ever watchful, the silent protectors of a legend they had carefully crafted, knowing it would outlive them all.

As dusk fell over the quiet mountain town of Berghold, the Guard slipped into the shadows, their movements practiced and careful. The atmosphere in this remote settlement felt different from the villages they'd visited before. Berghold was secluded, surrounded by mist-laden mountains that towered on all sides. This isolation made the town ripe for the next phase of the Guard's carefully woven deception.

The Guard gathered in a clearing just outside the town, hidden from view by the dense trees and heavy fog. Santiago motioned to his team, his expression serious as he outlined their strategy.

"Tonight, we plant a new seed," he began. "This time, we shift the story to a different location entirely—a mountain cave hidden in the peaks beyond Berghold. It's remote and treacherous, far enough that most will hesitate to venture there. But the reformists are desperate. We know they'll take the bait."

Emmanuel nodded, understanding the nuances of Santiago's plan. "If they hear of yet another hiding place, especially one so challenging to reach, it'll fuel their determination and paranoia. By scattering these rumors, we keep them from drawing too close to the monastery."

Isabela added thoughtfully, "And as they move from place to place, we reinforce the myth of the Codex's unapproachable nature. It's not just a legend; it's becoming a test—one they are constantly failing."

The team agreed, each member knowing their role. Santiago and Rafael would handle the reconnaissance and identification of any reformist scouts who arrived. Isabela and Emmanuel would enter the town, carefully spreading whispers among locals, dropping hints that would spark curiosity and lure the reformists into their trap.

With a final nod from Santiago, the Guard split up, fading into the night to set their plan into motion.

Isabela and Emmanuel moved purposefully through the cobblestone streets of Berghold, their faces partially hidden by hoods. The town's locals watched them warily, casting sidelong glances as they walked past. Though the town was small, its people seemed naturally suspicious, as if the harsh, isolated landscape had made them cautious of outsiders. It was the perfect environment to sow the seeds of intrigue.

In the corner of a crowded tavern, Isabela leaned in close to a group of townsfolk, her voice low but carrying enough weight to be overheard. "They say there's a hidden place deep in the mountains," she murmured, her eyes wide, as though imparting a precious secret. "A cave, untouched for centuries, where the old relic lies waiting for those who dare to seek it."

A man at the table raised an eyebrow, his expression skeptical yet curious. "A relic, you say?" His voice was gruff, lined with the accents of the mountain folk.

Emmanuel, seated nearby, added his own voice to the story. "They say it's no ordinary relic. It holds power, secrets. But it's cursed. Those who go looking for it don't come back. Not in one piece, anyway."

Another villager, an older woman with silver hair and a shawl wrapped tightly around her shoulders, shuddered. "We've heard of things like that up here—places better left undisturbed. The mountain keeps its own secrets."

Emmanuel leaned in slightly, casting a cautious glance around, as if fearful of being overheard. "That may be wise. My sister once knew a man who went searching in those peaks, thinking he'd find something valuable. He returned with his mind shattered, muttering of voices and shadows that followed him."

Isabela nodded, her expression somber. "The Codex, they call it. A book of power, bound by forces beyond our understanding. It protects itself, drawing only those with pure intentions—if such people exist."

The whispers began to spread around the room. The townsfolk, while skeptical, couldn't help but feel a spark of intrigue, even fear. They exchanged uneasy glances, each expression more troubled than the last. The tale of a hidden relic, guarded by unseen forces, was taking root once again.

The seed was planted, and the Guard withdrew quietly, letting the rumor take on a life of its own. As they walked back toward the clearing, Isabela felt a sense of satisfaction. "This story... it's becoming something beyond us. They're beginning to fear it, as though it has a will of its own."

Emmanuel nodded, his expression thoughtful. "Fear is a powerful weapon. If they believe the Codex protects itself, it may deter even the boldest of reformists from seeking it. And if not... we'll be waiting."

The following day, Santiago and Rafael took up positions along a narrow mountain pass that led toward the rumored location. It was a treacherous route, lined with jagged rocks and steep drops. The perfect place for an ambush. The two of them blended seamlessly with their surroundings, their clothing mottled with dirt and foliage to match the rocky landscape.

They had spent hours in silence, watching the pass, until they finally spotted a group of four reformist scouts making their way cautiously up the trail. Each scout carried the signs of a hardened soldier—clad in dark clothing, their movements quiet and practiced. They were clearly here for more than curiosity; they were here to hunt.

Rafael's gaze met Santiago's, a shared understanding passing between them. This group would not leave the mountain. They were too close, too dangerous to let go. Santiago signaled for patience, waiting until the reformists reached a vulnerable section of the trail, where the rocky ledge narrowed, leaving little room to maneuver.

As the scouts advanced, Santiago and Rafael moved with deadly precision, flanking them from both sides. Rafael drew his dagger, his steps silent as he closed the distance to his first target. Without a sound, he struck, his blade slicing across the scout's throat, ending his life before he could react. Santiago, on the opposite side, moved with equal lethality, his sword a flash of silver in the dim light as he dispatched another scout with a swift, practiced strike.

The remaining two scouts spun around, weapons drawn, but they were met with nothing but shadows and silence. Panic flashed in their eyes as they realized they were surrounded, outmatched by enemies they couldn't see.

One of the scouts managed to shout, "It's a trap! They're—" but his words were cut short as Santiago moved in, his blade finding its mark. The last reformist, realizing his fate, tried to flee, scrambling back down the path. Rafael was upon him in an instant, his movements swift and precise. Within moments, the scout lay still, the echoes of the struggle fading into the mountain air.

Santiago wiped his blade clean, his expression impassive. "They were too close. We can't risk even one of them making it back."

Rafael nodded, his gaze hard. "The reformists will grow suspicious soon, but they'll also grow fearful. The more we make it seem as though the Codex is guarded by forces beyond their control, the less likely they are to continue pursuing it."

They left the bodies in place, allowing nature to take its course. Any reformist who dared venture up this path would find the remains of those who had gone before them, a stark warning of the dangers that awaited those who sought the Codex.

Back in Berghold, word of the missing scouts spread rapidly. Villagers whispered of the men who had vanished on the mountain, some saying they had angered the spirits, others claiming the Codex had taken its toll. In a few short days, the legend had grown, gaining new layers as the locals added their own superstitions and fears.

Santiago and Isabela subtly encouraged the rumors, speaking to select individuals who would spread the tale further. They spoke of shadowy figures that guarded the cave, of voices that echoed in the night, warning all who approached. They hinted at supernatural forces, implying that the Codex's protectors were not merely human, but something more.

Emmanuel took to speaking with the travelers who passed through Berghold, dropping hints of the reformist scouts who had dared the mountain and never returned. He wove tales of an ancient curse that protected the Codex, warning those who were too eager to seek forbidden knowledge.

"The mountain takes those who go with greed in their hearts," he told one wide-eyed listener. "If you wish to see another day, it's best to let sleeping relics lie."

The listener shuddered, casting a wary glance toward the distant peaks. "Best to leave it alone, then. Nothing good comes from chasing secrets meant to stay hidden."

Each interaction left the townspeople more cautious, more fearful of the mountain and the Codex. The Guard's strategy was working; the reformists were growing wary, their numbers thinning with each failed expedition. Paranoia began to set in, whispers of betrayal and hidden dangers spreading among the reformist ranks. Some began to suspect that the Codex was indeed cursed, protected by forces they could not understand.

The Guard watched as their myth took shape, solidifying into something larger than themselves. The Codex was no longer just a relic; it had become a living legend, a dangerous pursuit that few would dare to follow. Every whispered warning, every vanished scout added to its mystique, creating an aura of fear that would deter even the most determined reformists.

As they prepared to leave Berghold, Santiago gathered his team, his gaze filled with quiet pride.

"We've achieved something powerful here," he said. "The Codex's true location is hidden behind layers of legend and fear. The reformists will hesitate, and with each new rumor we plant, they will lose more of their resolve."

Isabela nodded, a smile tugging at her lips. "We are not just hiding the Codex. We are transforming it into something untouchable, unreachable. A relic bound by mystery and guarded by fear."

Emmanuel's expression was thoughtful. "Legends have a way of growing, of becoming more than mere stories. If we continue this path, the Codex may become a part of history that only the foolish or the brave would dare pursue."

Rafael grinned, his eyes gleaming with satisfaction. "And those fools who do pursue it will find themselves met with… unexpected consequences."

The Guard departed Berghold, leaving behind a tale that would continue to spread, fueled by the villagers' imaginations and the reformists' desperation. They had become more than warriors; they were the guardians of a legend, protectors of a truth that transcended the physical.

As they traveled onward, Santiago felt a renewed sense of purpose. The Codex was not just a mission; it was a legacy, a symbol of faith and power that they would defend at all costs. They would carry on, weaving stories and planting seeds of fear, ensuring that the Codex remained protected, hidden within a labyrinth of myth and mystery.

For as long as they were vigilant, the Codex would remain safe—its secrets guarded by more than just men, but by a legend that no enemy could unravel.

In the heart of a dense forest, where the shadows were thick and only the faintest whispers of light broke through the canopy, the Guard gathered to assess the progress of their plan. Santiago had chosen the location carefully; a hidden grove nestled between towering trees, its floor covered with soft moss and fallen leaves that muffled every step. Here, they could speak freely, secure in the knowledge that no reformist spies would overhear.

The team sat in a loose circle around Santiago, who had spread a rough map of the region across a flat rock. The map was dotted with notes, marking towns where they'd planted rumors, ambush sites where reformist scouts had vanished, and paths that led only to false locations. Their campaign of deception had been remarkably effective so far, but Santiago's expression was unusually solemn as he reviewed their recent efforts.

Rafael broke the silence, his tone measured but tinged with satisfaction. "The reformists are running in circles. Every rumor we've planted seems to send them in a new direction. They're grasping at shadows."

Marco nodded in agreement. "The scouts we've intercepted didn't seem organized. They were desperate, unprepared, as if they're beginning to suspect they're being misled."

Santiago looked around the circle, his face a mixture of pride and caution. "Our strategy is working—perhaps even better than we anticipated. But I'm concerned about what this level of frustration might drive the reformists to do next."

Isabela leaned forward, her eyes narrowed in thought. "You think they'll escalate?"

"Exactly," Santiago replied. "We're dealing with more than just scouts or regular sympathizers now. They may bring in stronger forces, perhaps more skilled mercenaries or even leaders from within their ranks who wouldn't be so easily deceived."

Emmanuel crossed his arms, his face set in a contemplative expression. "The more we lead them astray, the greater their desperation will become. They've invested heavily in this pursuit—they won't simply abandon it. The reformists believe the Codex is their key to power, and each failed search will fuel their resolve. We need to prepare for what they'll do when they realize they're being manipulated."

Santiago tapped his finger on the map, pointing to Berghold and other nearby towns where they'd planted seeds of deception. "We've woven a complex web, and every part of it relies on secrecy. We can't afford even the slightest slip. The moment they sense a pattern or see through even one of our lies, it could all unravel. The Codex's real location is protected only as long as the reformists remain confused."

Rafael shifted, glancing around at the others. "If they do escalate, what can we expect? Organized raids? More scouts?"

"Possibly," Santiago answered, "but they may go beyond that. Reformist leadership may feel threatened by our growing reputation and could decide to move against us in ways we haven't anticipated. They could attempt to sow distrust among locals or try to root us out by any means necessary. It's even possible they might bring in specialists—assassins, skilled trackers—to hunt us down."

The group grew quiet as they considered the gravity of Santiago's words. It was one thing to deceive and eliminate scouts, but a targeted assault by a reformist cell determined to uncover the truth of the Codex's whereabouts was another matter entirely. They were few in number and couldn't afford a full-scale confrontation.

Marco broke the silence, his voice low and serious. "We're strong, but we're not invincible. If they start sending their best against us, we'll need to stay ahead of them, keeping ourselves just out of reach. Our strategy has to evolve with each move they make."

Isabela looked at Santiago, her expression resolute. "What do you suggest, Captain? How do we stay one step ahead?"

Santiago studied each of them, his gaze steady. "Our approach remains the same, but we must be meticulous. Every rumor we spread has to seem plausible but just out of reach. And from now on, we increase our mobility. We'll never linger in one location for more than a day or two, and we'll set up decoys to throw off any pursuers."

Emmanuel nodded thoughtfully. "If we create the appearance of multiple search parties or even spread conflicting rumors ourselves, it could add layers of confusion. Imagine if the reformists hear three different versions of where we're stationed at any given time. They'll never know what's true."

A glint of admiration flickered in Santiago's eyes. "Exactly. Our goal is to make it impossible for them to distinguish truth from falsehood. We need to create an illusion so complete that even the reformists doubt their own intelligence. And, more importantly, we must instill fear—not just of us, but of the Codex itself. Every encounter with us should reinforce the idea that the Codex is something far beyond their control."

Rafael cracked a faint smile. "If they're more afraid of the Codex than they are eager to find it, we've already won half the battle."

"True," Santiago agreed, "but fear can be a double-edged sword. Desperation drives men to recklessness. We'll need to keep our own actions unpredictable, changing routes, and doubling back if necessary. They'll be looking for patterns, any hint of our movements. We can't let them find one."

Marco leaned forward, tapping his finger on the map. "The mountain caves near Berghold might work for that. If we keep suggesting remote, hidden places, the reformists will keep stretching their resources, spreading themselves thin."

Isabela added, "And if we start leaving subtle signs of supposed 'supernatural' events—strange markings, odd sounds at night, the occasional trap—they might believe the

Codex has its own defenses, that it's resisting their attempts to claim it."

Emmanuel looked at Isabela, his smile approving. "That's clever. We're not just creating a false search but a series of obstacles that make each search feel more dangerous than the last."

Santiago glanced between them, nodding. "Yes, the Codex must be something more than a prize. To anyone who hears about it, it should seem alive, capable of protecting itself. They need to believe it's beyond their understanding or control. And our actions will reinforce that narrative."

The group fell into a thoughtful silence as they considered the plan's nuances. The level of deception and danger they were creating around the Codex was growing, but so were the stakes. Each false trail was not just a tactic but a legend in the making—a legend they needed to protect and perpetuate.

Finally, Rafael broke the silence, his expression grim. "We're committing to a dangerous game here. Each step we take leads us deeper into their sights. We're turning ourselves into the very guardians of a legend—one they'll stop at nothing to dismantle."

Santiago met his gaze, understanding the weight of his words. "Yes, but that's the choice we've made. We protect the Codex by any means necessary. This is no longer a simple mission; it's a test of our resolve, our willingness to stand in the shadows for the sake of something greater."

Emmanuel placed a hand on Santiago's shoulder, his voice steady and confident. "We're with you, Captain. This mission is no longer just a duty—it's a calling. We've already sacrificed much to protect the Codex. We're prepared to sacrifice more."

Santiago looked around the circle, meeting each gaze with unwavering determination. "Then let's be clear on what we face. From now on, we'll be moving through hostile territory, where every rumor we plant, every decoy we create, has to be flawless. There can be no slip-ups. Every move we make must serve the legend we're building, a legend so powerful that it keeps the reformists at bay."

A renewed sense of purpose settled over the Guard, binding them even tighter in their commitment. They were not simply warriors or guardians; they were the architects of a myth, protectors of an artifact whose legacy they would ensure survived the ages. They understood that their success depended on precision, skill, and the willingness to embrace the shadows.

"From this point forward," Santiago said, his voice resolute, "we are more than just men guarding a relic. We are the legend of the Codex, a force that cannot be seen or grasped. Every action we take, every rumor we spread will build a legacy of fear that will keep it safe."

They all nodded, their expressions solemn yet steadfast. The Codex's protection was now their life's work, a purpose that transcended their own lives and bound them together as something greater than a mere guard. They were keepers of a truth hidden behind shadows, a secret that would endure for as long as they remained vigilant.

With their renewed commitment, the Guard faded into the forest once more, shadows among shadows, knowing the path ahead would be treacherous but unwavering in their resolve. The Codex was no longer just a relic; it was the legend they would defend at any cost, a myth they would shape, a truth they would guard for as long as they drew breath.

**Chapter 5 - Arrival of the Zealots**

The Guard moved carefully along the edge of a small, sleepy village nestled between rolling hills and dense woods. The villagers bustled about their morning routines—gathering water, tending to livestock, sweeping porches—but there was a tangible tension in the air, as though the very ground held secrets that weighed heavily on the hearts of its people. Santiago gestured to his team to maintain their cover, their cloaks drawn low over their faces as they blended with the locals moving through the village square.

The Guard needed to be cautious. They had spent weeks planting false trails, eliminating reformist scouts, and carefully guarding the secrecy of the Codex's true location. But the energy of the village today suggested something different—a heightened sense of alertness that Santiago had learned to trust.

As they made their way closer to the village square, snatches of conversation reached their ears, drawing the Guard's attention.

"They say he's coming," an elderly man whispered to a group gathered near a well, his voice trembling. "The Viper himself, with his Zealots. They're searching for something… something the Church wants to keep hidden."

Santiago stilled, listening intently. He caught Rafael's eye, signaling him to remain silent but alert.

A woman shook her head, a mixture of awe and fear clouding her expression. "I heard his men are no ordinary soldiers—they call them the Zealots of Veritas. Fierce warriors, followers of Luther, each one trained to die for the cause. They say they can move like shadows and strike without mercy."

The words were chilling, and Santiago felt a ripple of tension pass through the team. The Viper's arrival would be no ordinary threat. His Zealots of Veritas sounded like a force trained and disciplined with a fanatical dedication, one that could match even the Guard's own skill.

Emmanuel leaned in, his voice barely a whisper. "If these rumors are true, Captain, this Viper could pose a greater challenge than any we've faced thus far. A man with a guard of devoted zealots won't be deterred by simple deception."

Santiago nodded, his mind racing as he considered the implications. "We need to gather more information," he murmured. "If the Viper truly intends to locate the Codex, we must understand his strengths and tactics before he gets any closer."

They moved into the heart of the village, careful to remain inconspicuous as they passed vendors and merchants peddling their wares. A group of men stood outside the tavern, talking in hushed tones, their faces pale with unease. Santiago slowed his pace, nodding to Isabela to drift closer and listen.

"The Viper's bringing destruction," one man muttered, his voice low and gravelly. "He claims he'll reveal the Church's secrets, tear it apart brick by brick."

Another man spat on the ground, his face twisted in disdain. "Good riddance, I say. The Church has held us down long enough. If the Viper can bring it down, maybe it's time someone did."

Isabela clenched her jaw, but she kept her face neutral, letting the men's conversation continue. The second man's sentiment revealed more than just fear—it spoke to the undercurrent of resentment and bitterness among the locals, resentment that reformists like the Viper had fueled to gain sympathy and support.

Santiago, catching Isabela's expression, felt a pang of concern. If the Viper was succeeding in winning the loyalty of the people, he could rally even more support to his cause, complicating the Guard's mission further. They needed to prevent the locals from siding with him, even if that required unconventional methods.

Moving to the edge of the square, the Guard found a sheltered spot under the eaves of a market stall. Santiago gathered his team, his voice barely audible.

"We need a strategy," he said, his gaze serious. "This Viper has the potential to draw followers simply by exploiting their resentment. If he builds enough support here, we could be looking at a full-scale uprising."

Rafael frowned, his brows knit in thought. "The Viper's men are likely trained as scouts, given their reputation. They'll be watching every move, listening to every whisper. The usual tactics won't be enough to stop them."

Marco nodded in agreement. "They won't be easily deterred by false rumors alone. And if their loyalty is as strong as we're hearing, they won't abandon the search until they have answers—or until they're forced to stop."

Santiago's mind worked quickly, a plan forming as he assessed their options. "We'll need to sow deeper seeds of doubt," he said. "If we can make them question the reliability of their own sources or the trustworthiness of their own mission, it might fracture their resolve. They can't report back what they can't verify."

The Guard fell silent, considering the gravity of the situation. This wasn't just about protecting a relic anymore—it was about confronting an ideology that had begun to take root in the minds of the people. The Viper wasn't merely a man hunting the Codex; he was a leader, a symbol of defiance against the Church, and that made him all the more dangerous.

Emmanuel spoke up, his voice steady but intense. "The Viper and his Zealots won't respond to reason or diplomacy. They're too far gone in their beliefs. The only way to stop them is to ensure they never find the Codex and to make it clear that this pursuit can only end in failure and ruin."

Santiago met Emmanuel's gaze, recognizing the unyielding resolve in his comrade's eyes. "Agreed. If we can turn the very rumors they rely on against them, we may weaken their focus."

They dispersed once more, each member of the Guard moving through the village, listening closely to every whisper and hushed conversation. By evening, they had pieced together a chilling portrait of their adversary.

The Viper was said to be merciless and cunning, a strategist who operated in the shadows and inspired devotion through fear. His Zealots were not just soldiers but ardent followers, disciplined and loyal, willing to die for their leader's cause. Each one was handpicked, hardened by years of training, and supposedly skilled in the arts of deception, making them formidable adversaries for even the most seasoned warriors.

As the sun dipped below the horizon, Santiago signaled the Guard to regroup in a secluded grove just beyond the village. His voice was grim as he relayed what they had learned.

"The Viper isn't coming here simply to search. He's coming here to conquer. If he believes the Codex is within reach, he'll stop at nothing to get it—and he'll bring the weight of the people's discontent to fuel his mission."

Marco's face darkened. "Then it's more than just a mission to him. It's a crusade, a movement he's using to rally followers."

Santiago nodded, his gaze sharp and focused. "That's exactly why we need to act decisively. We've led them astray so far, but this changes everything. The Viper's men are trained, yes—but they're also human. They're not immune to fear, and they're not immune to doubt."

Isabela met his gaze, understanding dawning in her eyes. "If we can make his forces believe the Codex is cursed or unreachable, we might plant enough seeds of doubt to make them question their cause."

"Precisely," Santiago replied. "We're not just guarding a location anymore. We're guarding a legend. Every story we spread, every rumor we craft needs to make this search feel not only futile but dangerous."

Rafael's eyes gleamed with determination. "If the Viper wants a war of fear and loyalty, we'll give him one. We'll make this mission of his look like a fool's errand, a path leading to ruin."

Santiago nodded, a hint of pride in his gaze as he looked at each of his comrades. "We'll act carefully and methodically. From now on, every move we make will carry weight. We'll exploit every shadow, every rumor. We'll spread tales of vanished men, of terrible retribution awaiting anyone who dares to come closer."

The Guard shared a silent understanding. They were more than warriors; they were architects of fear, guardians of a mystery so impenetrable that even the most loyal zealot would hesitate to pursue it.

As they prepared to leave the grove, Santiago placed a hand on Emmanuel's shoulder. "We'll need your insight, Emmanuel. The reformists have already turned many hearts. We must use every word, every hint to make their loyalty waver."

Emmanuel nodded, his expression solemn. "I understand, Captain. We'll do whatever it takes to protect the Codex."

And as the night deepened, the Guard set out with renewed purpose, ready to confront the Viper's forces not through brute strength alone, but through a weapon even more powerful—fear.

The Guard moved silently through the underbrush, keeping to the shadows as they neared the outskirts of a small town nestled among the hills. Santiago and Emmanuel, their cloaks blending into the dimness of early evening, crept forward to assess the enemy forces that had gathered there. This was no ordinary assembly; this was the Viper's personal guard—the Zealots of Veritas.

From their vantage point behind a dense thicket, Santiago and Emmanuel could see a series of tents set up in disciplined rows, each one marked with a crude emblem that looked like a serpent intertwined with a cross. The camp was orderly, almost militaristic, with clear paths between the tents, a central fire pit, and an area cordoned off for weapons and supplies. Santiago's eyes narrowed as he studied the layout, noting the tactical efficiency with which the Zealots had arranged themselves. This was the work of seasoned soldiers, not mere reformist fanatics.

Emmanuel leaned closer to Santiago, his voice barely a whisper. "They're as disciplined as we expected, Captain. No hesitation, no disorder. Each man seems to know his place and his role."

Santiago nodded, his gaze fixed on the movements of the Zealots as they prepared their evening meal. "This isn't just a gathering of supporters. These are trained warriors. If the Viper's goal is to retrieve the Codex and challenge the Church, he's chosen his men wisely."

As they continued to observe, Santiago noted the sheer dedication each Zealot displayed. They moved with purpose, their expressions focused and intense. There was none of the casual talk or laughter that one might expect around a campfire; instead, the men sat in quiet contemplation or spoke in low, reverent tones. Occasionally, one of them would stand and recite passages, likely from the teachings of Martin Luther, rallying their faith with solemn conviction.

Emmanuel's brow furrowed as he watched. "They're more than just soldiers; they're believers. This isn't just a job to them—it's a holy mission."

Santiago agreed, the weight of the situation settling over him. He had encountered many soldiers in his life, but these men were different. They were bound not only by loyalty to their leader but by a shared belief that what they were doing was righteous. That kind of faith could make men powerful—and dangerous.

As they watched, a figure emerged from one of the larger tents near the center of the camp. Santiago's breath caught as he recognized the man: tall and imposing, with a steely gaze and an air of authority that radiated even from a distance. This was the Viper, the mysterious figure whose very name had sent whispers of fear through the towns and villages.

The Viper's presence was magnetic, commanding instant attention. The Zealots ceased their activities, turning to face him with an almost reverential stillness. His dark cloak billowed as he strode confidently into the center of the camp, his voice carrying a quiet power as he addressed his followers.

"We stand here on the precipice of history," the Viper announced, his voice steady and unwavering. "The Codex Veritas holds the truth that the Church fears, the truth that will shake its foundations and bring down its walls. We are not here to merely seek relics. We are here to claim justice, to expose lies, and to free those who have been shackled by centuries of deception."

The Zealots responded with a silent nod, their eyes fixed on their leader with unbreakable devotion. Santiago felt a chill run through him as he watched. The Viper was not merely a leader; he was a symbol, a rallying point for these men who saw him as the embodiment of their cause.

Emmanuel's gaze was intense, his expression a mixture of concern and determination. "These men would follow him to their deaths without question. They're not here for plunder or glory. They believe they are fulfilling God's will."

Santiago's face hardened as he considered the implications. "Which means they won't be easily deterred. They're not just after the Codex for power—they see it as a divine mission. And that makes them a formidable enemy."

The Viper continued speaking, his voice laced with conviction. "We are not merely searching for a book. We are searching for a weapon—a weapon of truth that will destroy the falsehoods the Church has built its power upon. And each of you has been chosen because you have proven your faith, your strength, your loyalty to our cause."

He looked over his followers, his gaze piercing. "This is our moment. The Church has held power for too long, kept secrets for too long. But with the Codex in our hands, we will reveal the truth to all who have been oppressed."

Santiago exchanged a grim look with Emmanuel. The Viper was more than a strategist; he was a visionary, a man who had tapped into the discontent simmering among those who felt abandoned by the Church. The Zealots weren't just warriors—they were disciples of a new faith, one that saw the Codex as a symbol of liberation.

As the Viper's speech concluded, he motioned to a group of Zealots who were gathered near the weapons cache. One of the men stepped forward, presenting a map to the Viper, who examined it carefully. Santiago strained to see but couldn't make out the details from their distance. Whatever it was, it clearly held significance.

The Viper spoke in a lower tone, addressing the men directly before him. "Our scouts have confirmed whispers of the

Codex's location. We will move at dawn, and I expect each of you to be ready. Failure is not an option. We will strike with precision, with faith, and without mercy."

Emmanuel's jaw tightened. "They're planning an assault. If they've heard of our decoy locations, they might be led to one of the false trails we set up. But if they uncover the truth, if they realize the Codex isn't where they think…"

Santiago placed a hand on Emmanuel's shoulder, his voice calm yet resolute. "We won't let it come to that. We need to ensure that they remain in the dark, chasing shadows and rumors."

The Zealots began preparing for the morning's march, checking their weapons, reciting quiet prayers, and organizing supplies with the precision of veteran soldiers. Santiago couldn't help but feel a begrudging respect for the Viper's forces. They were not like the other reformist cells he had encountered—disorganized groups with loose allegiances. The Zealots were something far more dangerous: they were unified, disciplined, and unwavering in their purpose.

"Captain," Emmanuel murmured, breaking Santiago's train of thought. "If they're moving at dawn, we have little time to adjust our plan. We could intercept them on one of the false trails, lay another trap that would keep them away from the Codex for longer."

Santiago nodded thoughtfully. "That's our best option. We'll continue to lead them astray, but we must be cautious.

These men aren't easily fooled, and if they suspect we're playing them, they may redouble their efforts."

They observed the camp a while longer, noting how each Zealot moved with a quiet efficiency, their eyes sharp and alert even as they prepared for rest. These were men who had been tested, tempered by their belief and loyalty to their cause. They carried themselves with a confidence that spoke of both skill and faith, a rare combination that made them as dangerous as any opponent Santiago had faced.

As the camp settled into a hushed stillness, Santiago gestured for Emmanuel to follow him back into the cover of the trees. They retreated to a safe distance, taking care not to disturb the quiet of the night. When they were far enough from the camp, Santiago paused, turning to Emmanuel.

"We'll need to alert the others and set our ambush carefully. The Zealots are not to be underestimated. One mistake, and they'll uncover our deception."

Emmanuel nodded, his expression grim. "Understood. If the Viper is coming with this kind of force, he won't stop until he's certain the Codex is out of reach—or until he has it in his grasp."

Santiago's gaze was steely, his voice low and determined. "Then we make sure he never finds it. The Codex is more than just a relic—it's a symbol of knowledge and power that must be protected at all costs. If we fail, we risk not just the Church, but the very stability of the lands we've sworn to protect."

They moved through the woods with silent precision, their minds racing with the implications of what they had seen. The Viper and his Zealots were unlike any adversary the Guard had faced before. They were well-trained, fanatically devoted, and driven by a cause that saw the Codex as the key to their victory.

As they reached the outskirts of the woods, Santiago and Emmanuel shared a glance of understanding. This mission was no longer just about misleading their enemies or protecting a relic. It had become a battle of ideologies, a struggle to prevent the Viper from exploiting the Codex's power and reshaping the world in his image.

Santiago's voice was quiet but filled with resolve. "We know our path, Emmanuel. Let's make sure we see it through."

Emmanuel nodded, his gaze unwavering. "For the Codex. For the Guard."

And as they melted back into the night, their hearts were set on the path ahead, fully aware that this encounter would be unlike any they had faced before. The Guard would not only need their strength and skill, but every ounce of their cunning and faith, to outwit an enemy who believed himself to be on a divine mission.

The Guard gathered in a small clearing, the forest providing a natural canopy of shadows that concealed them from any prying eyes. Santiago surveyed his team, their expressions serious, each member fully aware of the challenge ahead. The Viper and his Zealots of Veritas were on the move, their purpose clear: locate the Codex and bring down the Church's influence. The Guard's mission had now become not only to protect the Codex but to ensure it remained a legend, a mystery that would elude even the most relentless of reformist forces.

Santiago began, his voice low but steady, as he outlined the stakes. "We're facing a formidable enemy—skilled, organized, and utterly devoted to their cause. The Viper isn't just sending a group of zealots to search for a relic. He's sending them to uncover what they believe is a weapon capable of toppling the Church. If they get any closer, they might start to unravel the truth."

Rafael, always focused and composed, nodded. "The Zealots of Veritas won't hesitate to scour every hill and valley to find it. They're skilled in combat, disciplined, and fanatical enough to sacrifice everything. That makes them a threat we can't afford to underestimate."

Emmanuel, who had observed the Zealots with Santiago, spoke up, his tone grave. "Their loyalty to the Viper is unwavering. They see him as a prophet, a liberator. These are men who will not yield, no matter how many of them fall. We need to plan for their resilience."

Isabela looked at Santiago, her eyes sharp and determined. "Then let's use their strength against them. The Viper's forces may be disciplined, but they don't know this terrain like we do. We can make every step they take more dangerous, every path they choose filled with uncertainty."

Santiago nodded in agreement, his mind working through potential strategies. "Our advantage lies in stealth and in our knowledge of this land. If we play our cards right, we can make them question every move they make."

Marco leaned in, an idea forming. "What if we set up a network of traps and distractions? Small diversions, enough to lead them away from the actual hiding place of the Codex. They'll be chasing shadows while we eliminate any scouts who stray too close."

Rafael's eyes gleamed as he added, "A series of misdirections. We could use traps, but also plant signs and symbols that hint at false trails. Anything that will draw them further into the wilderness and away from the truth."

Santiago considered this. "The Viper and his men believe they are on a righteous path, but if we create enough doubt and confusion, they'll start questioning whether they're being led astray. It won't take much to make them second-guess each step."

He looked to Emmanuel, whose understanding of terrain and tactics was unmatched. "Emmanuel, how quickly can you set up a system of traps in the paths leading to the nearby mountains? The terrain there is rough enough to make travel difficult without added obstacles."

Emmanuel nodded, his expression determined. "I can place a series of snares and pitfalls. Nothing obvious—these will be subtle traps that the Zealots won't spot until it's too late. I can also disguise the trails leading further into the hills. If they pursue, they'll find themselves deeper in the wilderness, far from any true location of the Codex."

Santiago approved, a sense of confidence building. "Good. We'll establish three primary points of ambush, each one near a possible 'Codex' site we've already spread rumors about. If any scouts arrive, we eliminate them quietly and leave evidence that reinforces the myth of the Codex's dangers."

Rafael tightened his grip on his sword hilt. "We can leave remnants of their supplies, perhaps even signs of struggle. It'll send a message to the others—that the Codex is guarded by forces beyond their understanding."

Isabela's lips curved in a wry smile. "Fear can be as powerful as any weapon. The more they believe the Codex is cursed or protected by divine forces, the more cautious they'll become. We need to plant those seeds and water them with every encounter they have with us."

Santiago's gaze swept over his team, pride welling up in him. Each member of the Guard was bringing their unique skill set to the plan, their experience and resolve forming a barrier stronger than any wall.

"Let's break down our roles," he said. "Emmanuel, as we discussed, you'll focus on setting traps along the routes leading into the mountains. Make sure there are no clear exits once they're in. Force them to either turn back or risk the hazards ahead."

Emmanuel nodded, his hands already moving to check his supplies for the task. "Consider it done, Captain. I'll make sure they don't see what's coming until it's too late."

"Rafael," Santiago continued, "you'll take Marco and set up ambush points around the most likely paths they'll take. When they come across one of our decoys, you make sure there's no one left to report back. Keep it silent, but leave enough evidence to stoke their fear."

Rafael's expression was resolute. "Understood. We'll make it look as though they encountered something… unnatural. Something that will make the survivors hesitant to continue."

Isabela added, "And I'll make my way to the nearby village to continue spreading rumors. Every story I plant will reinforce the dangers of pursuing the Codex. By the time they reach each false trail, they'll already be primed to believe they're entering cursed grounds."

Santiago felt a surge of confidence as he watched his team. This was more than a plan—it was a tapestry woven with precision, each member of the Guard contributing a vital thread.

"Remember," he said, his voice firm but carrying a note of caution, "the Viper and his men will be prepared for resistance, but they won't expect the level of deception we're about to employ. We need to be as elusive as shadows. If we're seen, it will unravel everything."

Marco's gaze was steady, his loyalty evident. "We'll be invisible, Captain. By the time they realize the truth, it will be too late."

With the plan set, the Guard prepared their equipment in silence. Santiago watched each of them as they checked their weapons and supplies, mentally readying themselves for the tasks ahead. This mission would demand everything from them—discipline, courage, and absolute unity.

As they prepared to part ways, Santiago spoke one final time, his tone solemn. "This isn't just about keeping the Codex safe. It's about protecting the people who would suffer if the Viper gained access to its power. We've sworn an oath to protect, to serve, and to guard the truth. The Viper may see himself as a liberator, but he's blinded by his own ambition. We know the price of such arrogance, and we know what must be done."

The Guard nodded, each of them reaffirming their commitment. They understood the weight of their mission, the stakes that went beyond their lives. This was about preserving a balance that had taken centuries to build, a faith that connected generations.

Emmanuel gave Santiago a firm nod, his voice steady. "We will not let the Viper lay his hands on the Codex. Not while we still breathe."

Rafael looked around at the group, his gaze determined. "The Zealots may be faithful to their cause, but they underestimate the power of loyalty born of service, not ambition. We don't fight for personal gain; we fight for something greater than ourselves."

Isabela's eyes shone with a fierce light. "Let them come. They may have their zeal, but we have truth on our side. And we will protect it with everything we have."

Santiago took in the resolve of his team, his chest swelling with pride. The Viper may have his followers, his carefully orchestrated plans, but he did not have the unity, the silent understanding, that bound the Guard together.

"Then let's begin," he said, his voice filled with quiet conviction. "May our steps be swift, our strikes be silent, and our purpose be unwavering."

They moved into the night, each member disappearing into the darkness with the quiet assurance of a shadow. Emmanuel went east, ready to set his traps and lay the groundwork for the Viper's forces to become ensnared in a labyrinth of confusion. Rafael and Marco moved north, scouting the paths where they would lie in wait, prepared to leave only whispers and fear behind. Isabela took a separate path, already forming the tales she would spread among the villagers to fuel the legends surrounding the Codex.

Santiago remained alone for a moment, his mind reviewing the details of their plan. He understood the risks, the razor-thin line they would tread between victory and disaster. But he also knew the strength of the team he led, their commitment to the cause, their unwavering loyalty to one another.

With a final glance toward the distant lights of the Viper's camp, Santiago melted into the shadows, his resolve as unyielding as the stone walls of the monastery they had left behind. The Guard's purpose was clear, their path set, and they would do whatever it took to protect the Codex and preserve the fragile balance of power.

As he moved forward, Santiago carried with him the words he had spoken to the Guard, a quiet mantra that steadied his heart and focused his mind: *They may come with zeal, but we guard the truth.* And he knew that, together, the Guard would defend that truth to their last breath.

The forest was silent, cloaked in the stillness that marked the hour before dawn. Hidden among the shadows, the Guard waited, their breaths held, their focus sharpened as they watched the small party of Zealots move along the narrow path below. Santiago's eyes followed each movement, analyzing their formations and their discipline. These were not ordinary scouts; each man moved with precision, their steps synchronized, their weapons ready.

Santiago signaled to his team with subtle gestures, the language of silence they had mastered through years of training. Emmanuel nodded from his position across the path, his posture taut and ready. Isabela and Marco were poised on the opposite side, concealed among the trees, with Rafael stationed slightly further down the path as a secondary line of defense.

As the Zealots advanced, Santiago studied their methodical approach. Each scout moved with an almost ritualistic focus, eyes scanning the shadows, hands never straying far from their weapons. These were men who had been trained to trust nothing, who relied on each other's instincts as much as their own.

In a low whisper that only his team would hear, Santiago murmured, "This is no ordinary group of scouts. Watch their signals; they move like one body, each anticipating the other's moves."

Emmanuel, crouched nearby, nodded. "They're disciplined, well-trained. They remind me of the soldiers we faced in Andalusia—the ones who didn't flinch even when they were outnumbered."

Santiago felt a faint pang of memory as Emmanuel referenced that battle, one of the skirmishes during their mission in Andalusia. The enemy soldiers had been fierce, loyal to a commander who had instilled unwavering discipline in them, just as the Viper had with the Zealots of Veritas. It had taken every ounce of the Guard's strategy and skill to overcome those soldiers, and even then, it had cost them dearly. Santiago's jaw tightened. This skirmish had the potential to be just as costly.

As the Zealots neared, the Guard tightened their formation. Santiago raised his hand, signaling the team to prepare for the ambush. When the first of the Zealots was within range, Santiago let out a sharp, quiet whistle—an agreed signal to begin.

Emmanuel sprang forward, his steps silent as he descended upon the first Zealot, his blade flashing in the dim light. He struck swiftly, disabling his target before the man could react, but the Zealots' discipline became immediately apparent. The fallen man's comrades reacted without hesitation, not a flicker of panic crossing their faces. In unison, they shifted into a defensive stance, weapons drawn, eyes sweeping the trees.

Isabela moved next, slipping out of the shadows to engage two of the Zealots simultaneously. Her movements were fluid, her strikes precise, but the Zealots countered with a skill that surprised her. Their movements were not only defensive but calculated, each of them taking small steps to prevent her from fully surrounding them.

She found herself locked in a swift, deadly exchange, her daggers meeting their swords in a rhythm that felt as much like a dance as a fight. In a brief moment, she caught Santiago's eye, a glimmer of acknowledgment passing between them. This was no ordinary fight—these were men trained in a style that matched the Guard's skill, a deadly symmetry that left little room for error.

On the opposite side, Rafael and Marco closed in on the other Zealots, their own strategies adapting to the resilience of their opponents. Rafael fought with a powerful, controlled precision, his strikes aimed to disarm or incapacitate, but the Zealots met each attack with counter-moves that showcased their training. They anticipated his movements, dodging and weaving, forcing him to adjust his tactics.

"This isn't working," Rafael grunted, ducking to avoid a sword aimed at his neck. "They're too disciplined—they aren't breaking formation."

Marco, moving swiftly beside him, grinned, a gleam of excitement in his eyes. "Then let's make them." With a calculated lunge, he feigned a retreat, drawing two Zealots toward him. As they advanced, he twisted his body, knocking one of them off balance and sending him sprawling.

Santiago saw the opportunity and seized it, moving in to capitalize on the momentary opening. His sword struck the exposed Zealot's shoulder, a disabling blow that forced the man to drop his weapon. But before he could press the advantage, another Zealot was upon him, moving with a swift, almost uncanny precision that caught him off guard.

The skirmish grew more intense, the forest echoing with the clash of steel and the muffled grunts of effort. Each member of the Guard found themselves challenged in ways they hadn't anticipated, forced to adapt to the Zealots' unique fighting style. It was as if they were battling mirrors—each movement met with an equally skilled counter, each strategy anticipated and answered.

Isabela ducked under a sword swing, her breath coming in quick gasps as she assessed her opponent. "They're reading us too well," she called out to Santiago. "It's like they know our methods."

Santiago's mind raced, the urgency of her words sinking in. "They're disciplined because they've been trained like us. They're no ordinary foot soldiers—they're elite, just as we are." He parried a strike, his mind flashing back to that battle in Andalusia, where they had faced soldiers who had been prepared for every tactic the Guard employed. This was no different, yet the stakes were higher now, the enemy's purpose more dangerous.

As he turned to deflect another attack, Emmanuel moved in beside him, his movements a blend of efficiency and power. "They don't waver, Captain. It's like they're fighting for something sacred, just as we are."

Santiago met his gaze, a shared understanding passing between them. The Zealots were driven by their faith in the Viper's cause, just as the Guard was driven by their oath to protect the Codex. This was not merely a skirmish for territory or honor—this was a clash of beliefs, a battle for what each side held most sacred.

A sudden yell broke through the chaos as Marco managed to disable another Zealot, sending him sprawling into the underbrush. But before Marco could press his advantage, two more Zealots closed in, their movements coordinated as they drove him back toward the trees. Santiago moved to help, his blade flashing as he deflected their strikes, but he could sense the strain in his team. The Zealots were resilient, their discipline unwavering, their resolve as unbreakable as their formations.

Rafael, breathing hard, managed to strike down one of his opponents, his expression grim as he called out, "We've thinned their numbers, but they're still pressing forward. They won't stop until they're forced to."

Santiago knew he was right. The Zealots would fight until there was nothing left of them. They were relentless, their eyes burning with a conviction that echoed their own. But he could see the strain in his team's movements, the exhaustion that was beginning to creep into their limbs. They had faced challenges before, but this was different—a battle where every strike had to count, every move calculated with precision.

"We need to shift tactics," Santiago called out, his voice carrying a note of finality. "Draw them toward the narrow path. Emmanuel, set up a defense there. We'll funnel them into a tighter space."

Emmanuel nodded, moving swiftly to take up a position near the narrow path that led deeper into the forest. The Guard moved as one, retreating just enough to lure the remaining Zealots toward the choke point. The Zealots, driven by their belief in their cause, took the bait, advancing with unyielding determination.

As the first of the Zealots entered the path, Emmanuel struck with a force that belied his calm exterior, his blade meeting his opponent's with a fierce precision. The Zealot staggered, caught off guard by the sudden shift in strategy, and Emmanuel pressed the advantage, his movements a calculated blend of defense and offense.

One by one, the remaining Zealots were funneled into the narrow space, forced to fight on uneven terms. The Guard, though exhausted, held their ground, their unity and training allowing them to capitalize on the Zealots' momentary disorientation. But Santiago could see the toll the fight was taking on his team, the weariness that showed in their eyes even as they fought with unrelenting focus.

As the final Zealot fell, the forest grew silent once more, the echoes of the battle fading into the stillness. The Guard stood among the fallen, their breaths coming in gasps, their bodies marked with cuts and bruises that bore witness to the intensity of the skirmish. They had won, but the victory felt tempered, the cost heavier than they had anticipated.

Santiago looked at his team, pride and concern mingling in his gaze. "We've seen their strength, their resilience. The Viper's forces are more than a threat—they're a mirror of our own abilities, honed with the same discipline, the same dedication. We can't afford to underestimate them again."

Isabela wiped a trickle of blood from her brow, her expression solemn. "They fight for their beliefs, just as we do. This isn't just about the Codex for them—it's a crusade. They see it as a weapon to bring down everything we stand for."

Emmanuel, his breathing steadying, nodded. "They're skilled, but they're also fanatical. They'll keep coming, convinced that their cause justifies every sacrifice."

Rafael's gaze hardened, his voice low. "Then we'll have to be even more careful. Every engagement, every encounter needs to be calculated. They won't hesitate, so we can't afford to either."

Santiago felt the weight of his team's words, the truth of their observations settling heavily on his shoulders. The skirmish had been a warning, a glimpse into the challenge that lay ahead. The Zealots of Veritas were not just soldiers—they were warriors of faith, bound to the Viper's vision with a loyalty that rivaled their own dedication to the Church.

He looked at each of them, his resolve unwavering. "This is only the beginning. They'll keep coming, and we'll need to be ready for every move they make. Our strength lies in our unity, our discipline. If we falter, even for a moment, they'll exploit it."

Marco, his voice firm, added, "Then we stay vigilant. We don't let them see our weaknesses. We fight as one, and we protect the Codex, no matter the cost."

As they moved to regroup, Santiago felt a quiet determination settle over him. The Zealots had proven themselves formidable, but the Guard had faced insurmountable odds before. This was a battle of beliefs, a clash of loyalties that would demand everything from them. But he knew that, together, they would face whatever challenges the Viper's forces brought.

The echoes of Andalusia, of battles fought and won with sacrifice and resilience, lingered in his mind. This skirmish was but one part of a greater conflict, a mission that would test them to their core. But Santiago knew that, for the sake of the Codex and all it represented, they would stand firm, united by a purpose that transcended fear.

They moved into the forest, their steps silent, their minds focused. The path ahead was fraught with danger, but the Guard would face it with unbreakable resolve, their loyalty to one another and to their mission as steadfast as the mountains that shielded their path.

The Guard regrouped in a secluded hollow, hidden deep within the forest. The trees around them stood tall and silent, offering a shield from prying eyes, yet the weight of secrecy pressed heavily on their shoulders, a constant reminder of the stakes they bore. As they settled into their hiding spot, the aftermath of the skirmish lay heavy on each of them—the lingering tension, the toll of battle, and the haunting realization of just how relentless their enemy was.

Santiago scanned the group, his eyes lingering on each member in turn, noting their exhaustion, the fresh cuts and bruises marking their skin. He felt a familiar pang of responsibility, a sense of duty not only to the mission but to each of them. It was his role to keep them safe, yet their purpose demanded risks that no amount of careful planning could avoid.

Emmanuel leaned against a tree, his breathing steady but strained. He broke the silence first, his voice low. "They're not just determined; they're unwavering in their loyalty. It's like fighting shadows—no matter how many we eliminate, more will come."

Isabela nodded, brushing a hand over a scratch on her cheek, her expression thoughtful. "They don't fear us. They don't even hesitate. Their dedication is… absolute. I haven't seen anything like it, not even from some of the most devout soldiers we've faced before."

Santiago exhaled, his voice calm but carrying the weight of his thoughts. "That's what makes them dangerous. They're not after wealth or fame; they're after something they believe is bigger than themselves. They see the Codex as the key to their victory, and nothing we do will sway them from that belief."

Rafael, ever the realist, crossed his arms, a hint of frustration in his tone. "But they have an advantage we don't: numbers. We're few, and we're scattered. Every fight drains us, every encounter leaves us more exposed."

The group fell silent at his words, the truth of them sinking in. The weight of secrecy, of maintaining the hidden nature of their mission, was beginning to strain them in ways that went beyond mere physical fatigue. The Codex demanded complete protection, a secrecy so deep that not even the Church's inner ranks knew of the Guard's full involvement. They were alone in their fight, every encounter a risk that the Viper's forces might discover not only the Codex's location but the Guard's role as protectors.

Santiago moved to where Rafael stood, placing a reassuring hand on his shoulder. "I know it's difficult. Every time we engage them, we risk exposing ourselves, and with it, the Codex. We can't afford to slip, not even once."

Marco, who had been quietly listening, finally spoke, his voice tinged with a mixture of frustration and loyalty. "Captain, with respect, I understand the importance of secrecy, but at what point do we need to consider asking for reinforcements? I know we can't compromise the mission, but we're facing an army with a handful of warriors. How much longer can we keep doing this?"

Santiago met his gaze, seeing the earnestness in Marco's eyes, the strain of a warrior who understood the weight of what they were doing but couldn't ignore the toll it was taking. "I understand your concern, Marco. Believe me, I've thought about it. But we must remember that secrecy is our only weapon right now. If we reveal the Codex's location to others, even those we trust, we only increase the chance of it falling into the wrong hands."

Emmanuel, standing nearby, nodded in agreement. "The Codex isn't just a relic. Its purpose, its power—it's something most wouldn't understand, something that could easily be misused even with the best intentions. We're not just fighting to keep it out of the Viper's hands; we're fighting to ensure that it remains safeguarded for the right reasons."

Isabela added, her voice steady but resolute, "It's difficult, yes, but the fewer who know about the Codex, the better. We are the only line of defense that can guarantee its protection. If that means facing greater risks, then we do so because it's what we signed up for."

The group fell silent again, each of them absorbing the words, the reality of their mission settling once more on their hearts. The Viper's forces were relentless, determined, and their pursuit only seemed to intensify with each passing day. It was as though they were fighting not just to protect an artifact, but to protect a secret that, if revealed, could alter the fabric of everything they held dear.

Santiago took a deep breath, his gaze firm as he addressed them. "Our duty is clear, and so are the risks. We knew this mission wouldn't be easy. And I won't deny that secrecy can feel like an added weight, especially when it forces us to face this enemy alone. But if the Codex falls into the wrong hands, if even a fragment of its knowledge is misused, it could have catastrophic consequences."

Rafael's expression softened, his understanding of the stakes clear. "Then we move forward. We can't let their numbers or their discipline shake us. We face what's ahead with a clear focus and without hesitation."

Santiago nodded, appreciating the resolve that returned to Rafael's gaze. He glanced at Isabela, Marco, and Emmanuel, each of them meeting his gaze with a quiet understanding, a determination that transcended words. They had all faced incredible challenges before, but this was different. This was a mission that required more than physical strength—it demanded resilience, faith, and a relentless dedication to a cause they could never fully share.

"From this point on," Santiago continued, "we operate with absolute caution. Every move, every encounter is carefully planned. We take no unnecessary risks. If the Viper's men are relentless, then we must be invisible—striking only when we must, then disappearing without a trace."

Marco's lips curved into a faint smile. "Like ghosts."

Santiago nodded. "Exactly. We'll be like shadows in the dark, striking only when it serves the mission. They'll fear us, but they'll never find us."

Isabela spoke up, her tone steady but with a note of warmth. "Our strength isn't in numbers—it's in our purpose, our unity. We are a team, a family bound by a loyalty that few could understand. That's what the Viper's forces lack. They may be devoted to their cause, but they don't have the bond we share. That's our strength."

Emmanuel gave her a nod of agreement. "We're more than soldiers. We're guardians. And that means we carry the weight of this mission together. Every risk, every battle, we face it as one."

Their words seemed to settle the atmosphere, bringing a sense of calm, a reminder of the unity they had cultivated over the years. It was this bond, this unbreakable trust, that had allowed them to face impossible odds time and again. And though the Viper's forces were relentless, the Guard was bound by something that no enemy could take from them.

Santiago looked at his team, feeling a renewed sense of purpose. "We've chosen this path, and we'll see it through. Our loyalty isn't just to the Codex; it's to each other and to everything we stand to protect. The Viper's forces may come in numbers, but they'll never match the strength of a team forged in purpose and faith."

The Guard nodded, each of them steeling themselves for what lay ahead. They had been pushed to their limits, but they were not broken. The mission's weight may have been heavy, but it was a weight they bore together, bound by a cause that demanded everything they had.

As they dispersed, moving to their separate positions to prepare for the next phase of their strategy, Santiago felt a sense of calm settle over him. They were outnumbered, their enemy tireless, but they had faced such odds before. Their loyalty was their armor, their unity their shield.

And as the dawn broke over the forest, casting a pale light through the trees, Santiago knew that no matter how relentless the Viper's forces became, the Guard would remain steadfast. They would protect the Codex with every fiber of their being, their secrecy a shield as powerful as any blade.

In the quiet morning light, they disappeared into the shadows, becoming the invisible defenders of a secret that would remain guarded, no matter the cost.

**Chapter 6: The Final Stand**

The dawn light filtered through the thick canopy surrounding the monastery, casting a muted glow over the quiet landscape. The Guard moved like wraiths through the dense trees and rocky outcrops that surrounded the monastery. Every step was calculated, every sound muffled, as they took up positions in the shadows, watching the advancing Zealots with cold focus. Santiago had chosen this terrain carefully, knowing that the thick foliage and uneven ground would give them the upper hand. It was not a battlefield that would favor brute strength but one that demanded stealth, patience, and precision—all qualities the Guard had mastered.

As the Zealots moved forward, Santiago signaled to the team, his hand gestures sharp and efficient. They each understood their role, and with a final glance, they spread out, each disappearing into the shadows.

Santiago's plan was clear: hit them hard and fast, then melt back into the darkness. The Zealots would be forced to second-guess their every step, unsure if they were walking into another ambush. Each strike would cost the Zealots more than just lives—it would cost them confidence, and Santiago knew that was as valuable a weapon as any.

Emmanuel crouched behind a thick tree trunk, watching as a group of three Zealots approached cautiously, their eyes scanning the surroundings with disciplined precision. He admired their formation, their rigid discipline; these were no ordinary soldiers. He could see the faint glint of armor beneath their cloaks, the flash of a cross medallion on each chest, signifying their allegiance to Martin Luther's cause and their role as Zealots of Veritas.

He waited, motionless, watching their footfalls and noting their rhythm. The Zealots moved in near-silence, their steps mirroring each other's, as if in sync with a single heartbeat. Emmanuel took a slow, measured breath, his fingers tightening around the hilt of his blade. Timing was everything.

In a swift, silent motion, he struck. Stepping out from the shadows, he drove his blade cleanly into the neck of the first man before retreating just as swiftly, vanishing into the trees. The second Zealot barely had time to react, a gasp escaping his lips as he tried to track Emmanuel's position. But Emmanuel was already gone, leaving only a rustle of leaves in his wake.

The remaining two Zealots tensed, their composure slightly shaken. One called out, but there was no response, only silence. The Guard's tactic had worked; the remaining Zealots hesitated, unsure of where to turn, and in that pause, Marco struck from another angle, swiftly and decisively. By the time the last Zealot realized he was alone, the Guard had melted back into the forest, leaving only the faintest trace of their presence.

Meanwhile, Santiago and Isabela worked their way along a narrow ravine, setting up a line of simple but effective traps. Santiago had rigged several tripwires that would trigger small rockslides down the incline, intended to disrupt the Zealots' progress and force them into disadvantageous positions. Each trap was meant not only to inflict physical harm but also to create psychological warfare, to make the enemy wary of every step.

The Zealots soon encountered the first trap. A footfall on a well-hidden tripwire sent a cascade of rocks tumbling down onto them. They scrambled for cover, one man going down with a cry as he was struck by falling debris. The others moved quickly to regroup, their formation rattled but holding firm.

Isabela watched from her concealed position, her gaze sharp as she tracked their reactions. "They're resilient," she whispered to Santiago. "They don't falter easily, even under pressure."

Santiago's expression was grim. "They're trained to endure. But even the most disciplined soldier can be worn down. If we make them doubt their surroundings, we'll have the advantage."

He motioned for Isabela to follow as they repositioned, blending seamlessly into the shadows once more. They moved quickly to another vantage point, knowing the Zealots would continue advancing, searching for a threat they could not see.

Rafael, stationed further along the path, observed as another group of Zealots approached. They had already fallen into a cautious, slow-paced rhythm, each step an exercise in vigilance. He admired their discipline, even as he prepared to break it.

He unsheathed his dagger, waiting until the group had passed him before striking. Rafael lunged forward, taking down the last man silently, then retreated into the shadows. The other Zealots noticed their comrade's absence only moments later, their cohesion slipping as they adjusted to the new threat.

One Zealot, his face a mask of controlled fury, called out a challenge, his voice low but steely. "Come out and face us! You hide in shadows, but your cowardice cannot protect you forever."

Rafael smirked, remaining hidden, knowing that silence was a more effective weapon than words. The tension built as the Zealots waited for a response, their nerves stretched taut by the invisible threat that surrounded them. This was no battlefield of honor—it was a war of attrition, one in which Rafael knew every advantage lay with the Guard.

As the day wore on, the Guard continued their relentless guerrilla strikes, each attack precise and brutal. They struck from behind rocks, from trees, from hidden alcoves. Each ambush lasted only moments, the Guard vanishing before the Zealots could react.

Yet the Guard felt the toll of the skirmishes. Their movements were growing slower, their breathing heavier. Small cuts and bruises from close encounters began to accumulate. Emmanuel, despite his stoic demeanor, winced as he felt the strain on his muscles. They had been pushing themselves to the limit, testing their endurance with every strike.

Between attacks, the Guard would fall back, regrouping in concealed positions to catch their breath and reassess. Santiago's gaze scanned his team, noting the weariness etched into each face.

"We're making progress," he said quietly, though his eyes reflected the strain of their efforts. "But they're not falling back. Each loss only seems to strengthen their resolve."

Isabela, her face pale but determined, nodded. "They're more than soldiers. They're believers, just like we are."

"Then we have to make them doubt their belief," Santiago replied, a steely edge in his voice. "The more they see their comrades fall, the more they'll question the wisdom of their mission."

Emmanuel leaned against a tree, breathing heavily. "These men are formidable, Santiago. They're unlike any enemy we've faced before. I expected them to lose morale, to waver, but it seems they are fueled by something more powerful than fear."

Santiago clenched his fists, his expression resolute. "Then we'll press harder. If they believe in their cause, let them see what true faith looks like. We cannot let them reach the Codex."

As dusk began to settle, the Guard initiated another wave of attacks, striking at scattered Zealots as they regrouped and prepared for another push toward the monastery. Marco set a fire trap that burst to life as one of the Zealots tripped a concealed wire, engulfing him in flames that lit up the forest. His comrades watched in horror, scrambling back as the smell of smoke and burning fabric filled the air.

The Guard continued their assault, using the confusion to their advantage. Rafael darted in and out of the shadows, taking down isolated Zealots with swift, brutal efficiency. But even as the Guard dealt blow after blow, the Zealots displayed a terrifying resilience, closing ranks each time a member fell, their grim expressions unyielding.

After the final skirmish of the day, the Guard regrouped in a dense grove, hidden by shadows and the thick underbrush. Emmanuel leaned heavily against a tree, his face slick with sweat and dust. He surveyed his comrades, noting their injuries, their exhaustion.

"These men are relentless," he muttered, his tone edged with respect and frustration. "We've cut down their numbers, but they remain strong. They don't break easily, Santiago."

Santiago nodded, wiping a trickle of blood from his brow. "I see that. Their discipline is as unwavering as ours. They're not just soldiers—they're as committed to their cause as we are to ours."

Isabela's voice was soft but firm. "We may be able to hold them off, but at this pace, we'll reach our own limits before they do."

Rafael glanced toward the distant monastery. "If they continue like this, they'll reach the Codex soon. We're fighting a battle of endurance, and they're matching us step for step."

Santiago looked at each member of his team, his eyes reflecting both determination and the weight of their responsibility. "We knew this mission would test us. We're protecting something that cannot fall into the wrong hands. And if we're the only thing standing between them and the Codex, then we will hold the line. We will fight until there is no breath left in our bodies."

Emmanuel straightened, a flicker of resolve hardening his expression. "Then we'll give them everything we have. Let them come; they'll see that no zealot can match the faith and fury of the Iberian Guard."

With that, they prepared for the next phase, knowing that they were nearing the final confrontation. Each member of the Guard was worn and battle-scarred, yet their resolve burned brighter than ever. They would protect the Codex, no matter the cost.

The Guard moved quickly and silently through the dim, ancient corridors of the monastery, each footstep filled with purpose. The weight of the coming battle hung over them, a palpable tension that seemed to thicken the very air they breathed. They had fought hard to protect the Codex, sacrificing their own safety time and again to keep it hidden from the zealots who sought to claim it. Now, in the heart of the monastery, they would make their final stand.

Santiago led the way, his face set in grim determination as he guided his team to the most defensible positions within the building. The monastery's architecture, with its narrow hallways and stone alcoves, lent itself to defense. He had walked these corridors for hours, mapping out every entry point and blind spot, ensuring that they had the best possible advantage for the battle ahead.

"Rafael," Santiago murmured as he stopped in front of a low archway leading to a narrow hall, "I want you here. This corridor is a natural choke point. They'll have to funnel through it to reach the inner sanctum. Use it to our advantage."

Rafael nodded, his expression resolute. "They'll regret setting foot in here, I swear it."

Isabela, standing nearby, glanced down the darkened corridor, her sharp eyes scanning the shadows. "I'll take the position above," she said. "If they reach this point, they'll be vulnerable from above. I can cover Rafael and slow their advance."

Santiago met her gaze and nodded, a quiet understanding passing between them. "Good. Marco and Emmanuel, you'll be stationed at the entrances to the sanctuary itself. We'll use the narrow stairwell to force them to fight us on uneven ground."

Emmanuel, his face calm but his eyes fierce, inclined his head. "We know this monastery better than they do. We'll make every step they take cost them dearly."

Marco tightened his grip on his weapon, glancing around the ancient stone walls with a sense of reverence. "We're defending something much greater than ourselves here," he said quietly. "This place—it holds more than just a relic. It's a testament to all those who have fought for faith."

Santiago placed a firm hand on Marco's shoulder, giving it a reassuring squeeze. "And we'll honor that legacy. Whatever happens here, we stand together."

They each took up their positions, moving with a mixture of calm efficiency and unspoken resolve. The atmosphere in the monastery was somber, as though the stones themselves sensed the gravity of what was to come. The Guard members moved to reinforce the entrances, using tables and shelves to barricade weaker points, while reinforcing the stone archways and narrow passages that would limit the number of attackers who could come at them at once.

As the preparations continued, the Guard took a moment to catch their breath, standing together in a quiet alcove where light filtered through a single narrow window. The silence was heavy, each of them lost in their thoughts, their minds flickering through memories of past battles and shared victories. For years, they had fought side by side, forging bonds stronger than blood. Now, they faced an enemy that rivaled them in strength and conviction, and the weight of that challenge was evident in each of their faces.

Rafael, who rarely spoke about his feelings, broke the silence first. "No matter what happens, I want each of you to know that it has been an honor serving with you," he said, his voice steady but filled with emotion. "We've stood against so many enemies together, and it has been the greatest privilege of my life."

Isabela nodded, her eyes filled with both pride and sorrow. "We have been forged in fire. Whatever happens here, I know our purpose was worth every sacrifice." She took a deep breath, her gaze settling on each member of the Guard. "Each of you is family to me."

Marco, ever the optimist, gave them a faint smile, though his expression was tinged with sadness. "If we make it out of here, I'll make sure we have a feast in every town from here to Rome," he said with a wry grin. "But if we don't... well, let's make sure the stories they tell of this day are worthy of legends."

Emmanuel, standing in the corner, looked at each of them with a quiet intensity. "We are more than just soldiers. We are guardians of a sacred trust, one that countless others have held before us. They didn't falter in their duty, and neither will we." He paused, his voice growing softer. "This mission—it's not just for us. It's for everyone who believes in the legacy we've protected all these years."

Santiago's heart swelled with pride as he listened to his comrades. They were not just soldiers—they were warriors bound by faith and a shared sense of purpose. He looked around at the team he had led through so many battles, feeling the depth of his responsibility to them. "We are the last line of defense. If the Codex falls, everything we have fought for, everything we believe in, could be lost. But if we hold here, if we stand together, we can ensure that this relic—and the hope it represents—remains safe."

The Guard nodded, each of them steeling themselves for the coming storm. They knew what was at stake, and though fear lingered in their hearts, it was tempered by an unbreakable resolve. They were prepared to give everything to protect the Codex.

As the quiet settled over them, each member of the Guard took a moment of silence, their thoughts turning inward. Rafael murmured a prayer, his head bowed as he clutched his sword. He had always drawn strength from his faith, and now, with the weight of their mission pressing down on him, he found solace in the words of the psalms. "The Lord is my rock, my fortress, and my deliverer," he whispered, letting the words steady his heart.

Isabela closed her eyes, focusing on her breathing as she calmed her nerves. She thought of her family, of her reasons for joining the Guard, and of the countless lives she had saved over the years. Her fingers brushed the rosary tucked beneath her armor, a reminder of the promises she had made to herself and to her faith.

Marco tightened the straps on his armor, his hands moving with purpose as he checked his weapon one final time. Despite his usual lighthearted demeanor, his eyes were serious, reflecting the gravity of the moment. He whispered a vow under his breath, a promise that he would give everything he had to protect his friends and the Codex.

Emmanuel knelt briefly, placing his hand on the cold stone floor. He had spent his life in this monastery, training in its halls, learning its secrets. Now, as he prepared to defend it with his life, he felt a profound sense of peace. He whispered a silent prayer, a final blessing over the monastery and all it represented.

Santiago watched his team, feeling a surge of gratitude for each of them. He took a steadying breath, his mind racing through the strategies they had prepared. Every plan, every tactic they had devised, would be tested in the battle to come. But he had faith in his team, in their skill, and in their dedication. Together, they would face whatever came.

Yet, the tranquility in the air did little to calm the unease that had settled over the Guard. Santiago, Emmanuel, Isabela, Rafael, and Marco gathered in the shadows near the entrance, their expressions tense. Signs of movement from the far hills had confirmed their worst fears: the Zealots had exhausted all the decoy locations and were now zeroing in on the monastery's true position.

Santiago knelt, "They're close. The false leads served their purpose, but now they've seen through them."

Emmanuel's brow furrowed as he looked toward the distant ridges, eyes scanning the slopes for any hint of the approaching enemy. "These Zealots are relentless. I'd heard tales of their discipline, but to watch them deduce each decoy... it speaks to their training."

Rafael tightened his grip on his sword, his gaze steely. "If they're this skilled at deduction, they won't falter easily here. They're aiming for the Codex as if it's a crusade."

Emmanuel nodded, his face reflecting both concern and determination. "If they reach the monastery, the traps will give them a taste of what lies in store. The original guardians of this place designed it to be a fortress of secrets, with every inch rigged to deter even the most skilled intruder."

He crouched beside Santiago, tracing a mental map of the monastery's defenses with his hands. "There are razor-thin tripwires, invisible pits concealed by stone slabs, arrows hidden in wall slits ready to shoot out with the slightest touch, and pressure plates that trigger collapses. Each trap was designed to halt any who dared enter unbidden."

Isabela's gaze remained fixed on the faint signs of movement in the distance, her expression determined but wary. "The traps will slow them down, but if they're as skilled as we suspect, they may navigate through more of them than we'd like."

"They're not just soldiers; they're fanatics," Marco added. "For them, this is likely a holy mission. A few lost men won't stop them."

Santiago nodded. "We need to prepare for the worst—that they'll get closer than we'd like. We're facing a formidable enemy, one as cunning and disciplined as we are. The only difference is, they believe they're ordained to find the Codex and use it for their cause."

Emmanuel's eyes hardened as he spoke. "We can't underestimate them. They may even know how to spot traps just by instinct. The Zealots didn't come this far by luck; they've studied every monastery and codex in their path. They know what to look for."

A ripple of movement at the base of the hill confirmed their suspicions. Several figures emerged, moving in disciplined formation. As they drew closer, they were forced into a line, the rugged terrain and dense forest pushing them to follow a narrow path toward the monastery's entrance.

From their concealed vantage point, the Guard watched as the first trap was triggered: a stone slab that looked like solid ground but gave way when stepped on. One of the Zealots stumbled, his foot plunging through the deceptive cover and triggering a series of quick, concealed darts that shot from a nearby crevice. The man fell silently, clutching at the darts embedded in his side, but before his comrades could retrieve him, another Zealot in line signaled for them to press on, bypassing the trap with eerie calm.

"They're prepared to make sacrifices," Santiago muttered, more to himself than anyone else. He watched the remaining Zealots maneuver around the collapsed stone slab without hesitation, as if they had anticipated the trap's presence. "But their discipline—look how they didn't falter, even after losing a man."

Emmanuel clenched his jaw. "I expected some of them to make it through the outer defenses, but not with such ease. They'll likely encounter the arrow traps further in. Let's see how they fare with those."

The Guard waited, eyes trained on the approaching party as they neared the arrow slit traps. These small openings in the stone walls were positioned to release arrows once triggered by any weight placed on the hidden pressure plate nearby.

The Zealots advanced cautiously, their leader holding up a hand as he observed the surrounding rock and uneven ground. Emmanuel felt a surge of anxiety as he watched the leader drop to one knee, examining the stone path before him. Then, as though he could sense the presence of the pressure plate, the man signaled to his comrades to step around it. Each soldier followed suit, avoiding the trap with precision.

"They're almost unnervingly aware," Isabela murmured, a trace of awe mixed with frustration in her voice.

Santiago's jaw tightened as he looked at his team. "This is beyond natural caution—they've been studying monastery defenses. Each step they take closer to the Codex is proof of how much of a threat they are."

Marco, watching the Zealots with mounting concern, nodded. "They're as relentless as we are, if not more. Their determination is unsettling."

Santiago observed the Zealots' movements with steely focus. "They're using each fallen man as an opportunity to learn. Every triggered trap gives them information that they use to maneuver around the next one. We're facing not just a group of zealots but trained tacticians."

As the Zealots neared the inner defense line, Santiago motioned for the Guard to retreat slightly, away from their vantage point. "Let's fall back a bit. We'll let the traps slow them as much as they can. But we'll need to engage them directly before they reach the inner sanctum."

Emmanuel nodded, his face grave. "We'll be dealing with a smaller force if we can draw them through the worst of the traps, but each man they lose only seems to fuel their resolve. By the time they reach us, they'll be like wolves cornered in a hunt."

The Guard shifted further back into the monastery, preparing themselves for the inevitable confrontation. Emmanuel moved alongside Santiago, his face betraying a hint of worry. "These men are more skilled than I anticipated. If they reach the Codex chamber, the traps within will be our last line of defense. But if they've been able to bypass so many already... we may need to prepare for hand-to-hand combat."

Rafael's eyes were hard with resolve. "We'll be ready for them, Emmanuel. They may be disciplined, but we're no less dedicated."

Isabela placed a steadying hand on Emmanuel's arm. "We've protected secrets before, ones that people would have died for. This Codex... it may be more powerful than anything we've encountered, but our resolve has never faltered."

Emmanuel's worry melted into a determined smile. "Then we're prepared. Let them come. But don't underestimate them. Every moment they close in is a test of our defenses and our will."

The sounds of the Zealots' disciplined footsteps grew louder as they approached, echoing through the stone corridors with an ominous rhythm. The Guard could feel the pressure mounting, a reminder that each step taken by the Zealots meant one step closer to the Codex and the knowledge they sought to protect.

"We'll hold the line," Santiago said, his voice a calm command that steadied the team. "They may think they've faced danger, but they've yet to face us. Remember, our purpose is not just in the battle but in keeping what's within these walls safe. Today, we prove that purpose."

The Guard took their positions, each member bracing for the impending clash with the Zealots. The air felt thick with anticipation, every heart pounding with the knowledge that this would be a battle unlike any they'd faced. The Zealots' training and discipline matched their own, but it was their mission—their purpose—that would set the Guard apart.

As the final sounds of the Zealots' advance drew near, the Guard steeled themselves. They would meet the Zealots with the full force of their skills and the unwavering dedication that had carried them this far. This confrontation, they knew, was a test not just of strength but of will, as they fought to protect the Codex from falling into the hands of those who would use it for destruction.

The quiet tension solidified into a fierce resolve. The Guard was ready.

They moved to their designated spots, each taking up position in the darkened corridors and hidden alcoves that lined the monastery's heart. The silence was absolute, broken only by the faint rustling of armor as they adjusted their stances and waited.

The air was thick with tension, the knowledge that this could be their last battle hanging heavy over them. Yet, within that tension was a fierce determination, a shared understanding that they were willing to give everything to protect what they had sworn to defend. The Guard was ready—ready to fight, to protect, and if necessary, to lay down their lives for the Codex.

As the shadows deepened and the silence stretched, they waited, each heartbeat echoing the gravity of their mission. The Guard had fought countless battles, but this was different. This was the culmination of everything they believed in, a fight for faith and legacy, for the very soul of their mission.

And in that final moment of stillness, Santiago knew with absolute certainty that they would stand united, no matter what lay ahead.

The assault began with a thunderous crash that echoed through the monastery walls, shattering the stillness of the sacred hallways. Outside, the Zealots of Veritas had gathered in tight formations, their expressions hardened by their shared conviction and their loyalty to the Viper. This was more than an assault—it was a crusade in their minds, a divine mission to seize the Codex and destroy anyone who dared protect it.

Santiago stood at the monastery's heart, listening to the reverberation of each impact against the ancient stone walls. The weight of the moment pressed down upon him, but he knew that his team was prepared. They had fought countless battles together, and though this one might prove to be their last, they were united by purpose and unbreakable bonds.

The first wave of Zealots surged forward, their disciplined movements precise and powerful. They advanced in tight formations, shield walls up, creating a solid front as they charged through the corridors. Santiago's mind raced as he assessed their approach, noting the cohesion in their ranks and the unyielding resolve in their eyes.

"Hold the line!" Santiago commanded, his voice steady, carrying through the tense air. "Wait for them to funnel in—don't engage until they're in the choke points."

Rafael was the first to face the attackers. Positioned strategically at a narrow corridor, he watched the Zealots draw closer, their forms dark and intimidating. He tightened his grip on his sword, the leather-wrapped hilt grounding him in the moment. As the first Zealot moved into the corridor, Rafael lunged forward, his blade flashing as it struck with deadly precision. The enemy staggered, a look of shock momentarily crossing his face before he fell, and another took his place.

From above, Isabela provided cover, her crossbow loaded and aimed with deadly intent. She waited for Rafael to create an opening and fired, her bolt finding its mark in the shoulder of a Zealot who stumbled backward, allowing Rafael to press his advantage. Her position offered her an excellent vantage point, but it left her exposed. As she reloaded, a Zealot on the ground below noticed her perch and aimed his own crossbow in her direction.

"Isabela, watch out!" Marco's warning cut through the noise, and she ducked just as the bolt whizzed past her head, embedding itself in the stone wall behind her. Gritting her teeth, she took aim once more, returning fire and neutralizing her would-be assailant.

Meanwhile, Marco and Emmanuel held the eastern side of the monastery, where the Zealots were attempting to force their way in through a side passage. Emmanuel knew the monastery's layout better than anyone, and he used the narrow passageways to his advantage, luring the Zealots into cramped spaces where their numbers meant less. Each strike he delivered was calculated and efficient, the years of training evident in his every movement.

A particularly formidable Zealot with a scarred face and fierce determination stepped forward to face Emmanuel, his sword poised with deadly intent. Emmanuel matched the man's stance, his eyes calm and focused. They circled each other, the noise of battle fading into the background as Emmanuel focused solely on his opponent.

The Zealot attacked, his strikes swift and powerful, but Emmanuel parried each blow with precision, his experience giving him an edge. Their swords clashed, ringing through the stone halls as they moved in a deadly dance. Emmanuel noted the Zealot's aggressive stance, waiting for the moment his opponent's overconfidence would lead to an opening.

Finally, it came. The Zealot lunged forward, and Emmanuel sidestepped, twisting his blade to strike with pinpoint accuracy. The Zealot staggered, a look of shock in his eyes as he fell, his weapon slipping from his grasp. Emmanuel took a steadying breath, his gaze sweeping over the other advancing enemies as he prepared to continue the fight.

Santiago, stationed near the main entrance, observed the skirmishes, analyzing the Zealots' tactics. He could see that they were unrelenting, driven by an almost fanatical devotion. He called out commands to his team, directing their movements and adjusting their defenses to counter the attackers' strategy.

"Marco, fall back slightly and draw them into the corridor! Isabela, cover the left flank! Rafael, hold your ground; don't let them breach the second line!"

The Guard moved in sync with Santiago's orders, their movements honed from years of training and countless battles together. They fought as a single unit, each of them covering the other's vulnerabilities, turning the monastery's ancient corridors into a deadly maze for the attackers.

But the Zealots were tenacious. They pressed on, wave after wave, forcing the Guard to fight with every ounce of strength they possessed. Sweat poured down Rafael's face as he deflected another blow, his muscles straining under the continuous assault. A Zealot's blade sliced across his arm, drawing blood, but Rafael barely flinched, his focus unbroken as he pushed the attacker back with a fierce strike.

Isabela, from her elevated position, continued firing her crossbow, her bolts finding their marks with lethal accuracy. Yet, in the chaos, she didn't see the Zealot who had scaled the nearby wall. He lunged at her, and she barely had time to turn, blocking his dagger with her crossbow. The force of the impact jarred her, but she held her ground, wrestling with the attacker until she could draw her own blade and dispatch him.

The skirmish left her panting, her shoulder bleeding from a shallow cut. She glanced down to see Rafael, his own wounds visible but his expression determined. They shared a nod, a silent acknowledgment of their shared resilience, even as their injuries accumulated.

As the battle raged on, the Zealots showed no signs of retreat. Their discipline was unshakable, their formations tight and their movements coordinated. Each time the Guard managed to push them back, more surged forward, filling the spaces left by their fallen comrades. The narrow hallways were littered with bodies, both Zealots and defenders, yet the onslaught continued.

Marco, positioned at one of the secondary entrances, fought with a fierce intensity, his usual humor replaced by a cold focus. He moved with calculated precision, his strikes powerful and unyielding. Yet, even he was beginning to feel the strain. A Zealot's blade grazed his side, and he winced, the pain sharp but not enough to stop him. He gritted his teeth, pressing forward with renewed determination, each swing of his sword a testament to his loyalty to his comrades.

Emmanuel, despite his fatigue, continued to fight with a relentless focus. He observed the Zealots' disciplined formations and noted their weaknesses, exploiting them whenever possible. He positioned himself strategically, drawing enemies into vulnerable positions where he could dispatch them with efficiency. But he too felt the toll of the battle, the weight of each swing heavier than the last.

Santiago, watching his team fight with everything they had, felt a surge of pride mixed with grim determination. He knew they couldn't hold out forever—the Zealots' numbers were too great, their fervor too intense. But as long as his team stood, he would not yield. He joined the fray, his blade moving with precision and skill as he cut through the advancing attackers.

A Zealot charged at him, his face twisted in rage, but Santiago sidestepped, his blade flashing as he struck, the enemy falling to the ground. He moved with the confidence of a seasoned warrior, his every action calculated, his focus absolute. He knew that his role was not only to fight but to lead, to keep his team together and inspired in the face of overwhelming odds.

At one point, Santiago saw Emmanuel falter, a Zealot bearing down on him with a heavy axe. Without hesitation, Santiago moved to his side, intercepting the blow and pushing the attacker back. Emmanuel nodded his gratitude, a brief smile flickering across his face before they turned back to the fight, their backs to each other, guarding one another as they faced the oncoming wave.

As the battle stretched on, the monastery's stone walls echoed with the sounds of clashing steel, cries of pain, and shouted commands. The Guard fought with everything they had, their bodies battered and their spirits strained, yet their resolve remained unbroken. They were defending more than just a relic—they were defending a legacy, a mission that transcended their own lives.

The Zealots, despite their own losses, continued their relentless advance, their faith in their cause as unyielding as the Guard's. Yet, with every step forward, they paid a heavy price. The Guard's strategic positioning and use of the monastery's narrow corridors turned the Zealots' numbers against them, forcing them into close quarters where they could not fully utilize their formations.

But the toll on the Guard was visible. Rafael's arm hung at an awkward angle, blood staining his armor, though he continued to fight with a fierce determination. Isabela's face was pale, her breathing labored as she fired her crossbow, each shot taking a little more of her strength. Marco's movements were slower, his normally agile form weighed down by exhaustion and injury. Emmanuel, though tireless in his defense, was beginning to show signs of wear, his strikes slower, his breath heavier.

Santiago looked around at his team, seeing the toll the battle had taken on them. He felt a surge of anger at the Zealots' unrelenting fanaticism, their willingness to sacrifice everything for a cause that threatened all he held dear. But beneath that anger was an unshakable resolve. He would not let them take the Codex. He would not let his team's sacrifices be in vain.

As the Zealots pressed forward for what seemed like a final push, Santiago rallied his team, his voice cutting through the chaos. "Hold fast! We are the line that stands between them and everything we've fought for. We will not fall here!"

The Guard, battered and exhausted, found strength in his words. They tightened their ranks, preparing for one last stand, their eyes steely, their grips firm. They knew the stakes, and they knew that this was the moment they had trained for, the moment their lives had led to.

With a final surge of determination, the Guard stood united, ready to face whatever came, their loyalty to each other and to their mission unwavering. The final assault would test them to their very limits, but they were prepared to give everything—to fight, to protect, and, if necessary, to lay down their lives for the Codex.

As the Zealots surged forward, the Guard met them with unyielding force, their final stand a testament to their courage, their skill, and their unbreakable spirit. The battle was far from over, but in that moment, they knew that they would fight with everything they had until the very end.

The chaos in the monastery's final corridor had finally subsided. Bodies of the Zealots of Veritas lay strewn across the floor, their once impenetrable ranks broken. The Guard, though battered and exhausted, stood victorious, each of them bearing the marks of the brutal battle they had just fought. Yet, as the dust began to settle, a chilling silence swept over them. The fight was not over. From the shadows at the far end of the hall, a figure emerged—the Viper himself.

The air thickened as the Viper stepped forward, his stride slow and calculated, his eyes fixed on Santiago with an intense and unyielding gaze. His dark armor gleamed in the dim torchlight, and a faint, unsettling smile curled at his lips. He surveyed the remnants of his fallen forces, but there was no remorse in his expression, only a cold, fervent determination.

"So, who are you," the Viper sneered, his voice smooth yet laced with venom. "The supposed defender of secrets that should have crumbled under the weight of their own lies long ago?"

Santiago tightened his grip on his sword, meeting the Viper's gaze with calm defiance. He could feel the exhaustion in his muscles, the ache from every wound sustained in the prolonged fight, yet he stood tall, resolute.

"This Codex," the Viper continued, taking another step closer, "isn't yours to protect. It's a tool—a weapon meant to bring truth and revolution. What gives you the right to hoard it, to bury it in shadow while the world suffers under deceit?"

"It is not our place to wield such power as a weapon," Santiago replied, his voice steady. "This Codex holds knowledge that could uplift or destroy. Only those who understand the weight of that responsibility should even approach it."

The Viper laughed, a dark and mirthless sound that echoed through the blood-stained corridor. "Such noble ideals. But they mean nothing. The truth is meant to liberate, to reshape the world, not to be hidden behind walls of self-righteousness. You claim to protect it, but really, you're just afraid of losing control."

With that, the Viper drew his sword—a sleek, blackened blade that seemed to absorb the light around it. He raised it toward Santiago, his eyes glinting with deadly intent. "Let's see if your faith can stand against the truth."

Santiago squared his stance, drawing a steadying breath, and raised his sword to meet the challenge. "I can do all things through Christ which strengthens me."

They moved toward each other with deliberate steps, the space between them charged with the weight of their opposing beliefs. The Guard, still fending off the last scattered remnants of the Zealots, looked on with tense anticipation, aware that this confrontation would determine the fate of everything they had fought for.

The Viper struck first, his movements swift and controlled, his blade a blur as it sliced toward Santiago. Santiago parried, his arms vibrating with the force of the blow. The Viper was relentless, his strikes calculated to unbalance and break

Santiago's defense, his attacks infused with years of discipline and a zealot's conviction.

"You hide behind faith, behind duty," the Viper hissed, pressing Santiago back with each brutal swing. "But you're no different from the men you fight to protect—afraid, clinging to power that doesn't belong to you."

Santiago gritted his teeth, finding his footing and pressing back with equal force. "Faith is not a shield I hide behind. It's the foundation I stand on. The LORD is my strength and my shield; my heart trusts in him, and he helps me" He deflected a vicious strike and countered, his blade flashing as it grazed the Viper's side, drawing first blood. The Viper recoiled slightly, his eyes narrowing with fury.

"All the faith in the world won't stop the truth from coming to light," the Viper spat, ignoring the pain as he swung his sword again, aiming for Santiago's shoulder.

Santiago dodged, pivoting gracefully and bringing his own sword up to block. "Truth without wisdom is dangerous. You would wield it recklessly, bringing destruction to all you claim to save."

The Viper's gaze darkened, and he feinted to the left before lunging with renewed fury. Santiago barely deflected the strike, their blades locking, their faces mere inches apart. The Viper's eyes burned with fervor. "Better a world rebuilt from the ashes than one that rots in stagnation."

Santiago met his gaze, unwavering. "And you think you're fit to be its arbiter? The power to decide life and death, faith and ruin? That's not liberation—it's tyranny."

With a roar, the Viper broke the lock, launching a relentless series of strikes, his speed and aggression fueled by his unbridled conviction. Santiago felt the strain, each blow testing his resolve, each swing of his sword costing him precious energy. But he stood firm, his mind clear, his purpose steady.

Nearby, Rafael and Isabela fought to defend the entrance to the Codex's chamber, their movements slowed by their wounds. They kept the remaining Zealots at bay, even as their own blood stained the stone floors. Marco and Emmanuel fought tirelessly alongside them, each guard covering the other's blind spots, intercepting any threat that managed to slip past Santiago's line of defense.

The battle between Santiago and the Viper reached a fever pitch. The Viper's skill was undeniable, his strikes brutal and precise. Yet Santiago held his ground, his movements guided not by rage or desperation, but by a deep, abiding purpose. For each blow the Viper landed, Santiago returned one with equal strength, his calm and focus proving a match for the Viper's intensity.

"You don't have to die here," the Viper sneered as their blades clashed again, his voice a mocking whisper. "Swear loyalty to our cause, and I'll grant you a place in the new world. You're a warrior, don't waste your life on lost causes."

But Santiago's expression remained resolute. "My cause isn't lost. It lives in every life we protect, in every soul that chooses peace over chaos. I serve a purpose beyond myself—something you'll never understand."

With a final surge of strength, Santiago broke the Viper's stance, catching him off-guard. He pushed forward, his blade finding an opening in the Viper's defense. The Viper staggered back, blood staining his side as he glared at Santiago, his eyes blazing with a mix of rage and disbelief.

The Viper attempted one last desperate lunge, but Santiago sidestepped, his blade flashing in a decisive strike that disarmed the Viper, sending his weapon clattering across the stone floor. The Viper stumbled, weakened, his breath ragged as he sank to his knees, his eyes never leaving Santiago's.

Defeated but defiant, the Viper looked up, his expression twisted with scorn. "You think this changes anything? The truth will come for you, you can't hide it forever."

Santiago's gaze was steady, his voice calm. "It's not about hiding the truth—it's about honoring it with the wisdom it demands." He raised his sword, his movements slow and deliberate, his every gesture a testament to the unwavering faith that guided him.

With a single, swift stroke, Santiago brought an end to the Viper's rebellion, his blade finding its mark. The Viper fell, his expression one of frozen shock as his body crumpled to the ground, the life fading from his eyes.

The remaining Zealots, seeing their leader fall, looked on with horror. The once-unbreakable force faltered, their resolve shattered by the sight of the Viper's defeat. Some dropped their weapons, surrendering, while others fled, their faith in their cause dissolving in the face of overwhelming loss.

Santiago turned to the Guard, his expression somber but resolute. "The battle is over," he said, his voice carrying the weight of the struggle they had just endured. He looked at each of them in turn—Rafael, Isabela, Marco, Emmanuel—all of them marked by their wounds, but alive, their spirits unbroken.

Rafael let out a weary sigh, lowering his bloodied sword. "It's done," he murmured, a mixture of relief and exhaustion in his voice.

Isabela leaned against the wall, breathing heavily, her hand pressed to a wound on her arm. "For now," she said quietly, casting a final glance at the fallen Viper. "But we've sent a message. They won't come for the Codex again so easily."

Marco looked around at the remnants of the battle, his face etched with fatigue but also with pride. "We held our ground. We protected what needed to be protected."

Emmanuel, his eyes heavy with the memories of the fight, nodded. "It's not just about defending the Codex. It's about preserving something that transcends us all."

Santiago sheathed his sword, his gaze lingering on the fallen Viper. The battle had been hard-won, and the cost had been steep. But they had fulfilled their duty, standing against an enemy whose zeal had threatened to destroy all they had sworn to protect.

Together, the Guard gathered in silence, the weight of the moment settling over them. They had survived the Viper's assault, defended the Codex, and upheld the legacy they had been entrusted with. Their loyalty, faith, and resolve had seen them through, and they knew that their mission—their sacred duty—would continue.

For now, they could rest, knowing they had protected the Codex from those who would misuse its power. But they also understood that as long as the Codex existed, so too would the threat. They were guardians of something far greater than themselves, a truth they carried with honor, knowing that they would stand ready whenever they were needed again.

The air was thick with the scent of battle—sweat, blood, and the lingering trace of burning torch smoke. The monastery, once filled with echoes of clashing steel and the cries of combat, had settled into a haunting silence. The Guard gathered in a small chamber adjacent to the main hall, each of them bearing the weight of the fight and the injuries that came with it.

Isabela and Rafael, both wounded but alive, sat near a rough-hewn stone bench, their faces pale but resolute. Marco and Emmanuel moved between them, tending to wounds with practiced hands and whispered reassurances. Santiago, his gaze steady and distant, stood at the room's entrance, scanning their surroundings and keeping watch. Even in this moment of reprieve, his mind was already on the task of securing the Codex and fortifying their defenses.

Rafael winced as Emmanuel wrapped a length of linen around his arm, binding a deep gash he had sustained during the final skirmish. His usual lively expression was subdued, his brow furrowed in concentration as he held himself steady. "Feels like it's been ages since a fight tested me like that," he murmured, offering a faint smile to mask the pain.

Emmanuel nodded as he tightened the bandage, his movements gentle but firm. "The Zealots were unlike any opponents we've faced. Their resolve mirrored our own, in its own twisted way. This will take time to recover from," he admitted, though there was a quiet pride in his eyes.

Isabela leaned back, her own wounds tended to, though fatigue was evident in her face. "If they had been any less disciplined, we might have been able to avoid half the casualties," she said softly. "They fought not just for their leader, but for a cause. It reminded me of... well, of us."

Santiago turned from his post, his eyes thoughtful as he regarded his team. "It's true," he said, his voice filled with a mix of respect and solemnity. "In another life, perhaps they might have been our allies. They were as devout in their own way as we are, driven by faith and loyalty. But their belief was marred by ambition and zealotry."

Marco, who had been silently applying pressure to a wound on his shoulder, looked up and added, "The Viper's hold on them was strong. They believed in his vision of the Codex as a tool of revolution, a means to reshape the Church by force. In his mind, he saw himself as a liberator." He paused, his gaze distant. "The Zealots will regroup, if any are left. There may yet be those who will carry on his vision."

Rafael shook his head, a look of determination in his eyes despite the pain. "If they come again, we will stand against them, just as we did today. The Codex is more than words on parchment—it's a legacy, and it is our duty to protect it, to ensure it isn't twisted for personal ambition."

Santiago took a seat, finally allowing himself a moment to rest as he looked at each member of the Guard in turn. They were all battered, worn by battle, but there was a fierce determination in their eyes that told him their spirits were unbroken. "We knew this path would demand sacrifice," he said quietly. "Each of us took an oath to protect the Church, knowing the cost."

Emmanuel spoke up, his tone calm but resolute. "This battle may be over, but we cannot be lulled into complacency. The Viper may have fallen, but he wasn't the only one seeking the Codex. His defeat will inspire whispers, and those whispers will attract others—powerful individuals who believe they, too, are worthy to wield its knowledge."

A contemplative silence filled the room as his words sank in. They all knew the truth of his statement. The Codex was not a prize to be won and forgotten; it was a beacon, drawing the ambitious, the righteous, and the desperate alike.

Isabela broke the silence, her voice quiet but firm. "This mission never truly ends, does it?" She glanced around, her gaze lingering on each of her comrades. "We'll always be looking over our shoulders, waiting for the next Viper, the next zealot who thinks the Codex is theirs to take."

Santiago placed a reassuring hand on her shoulder. "Perhaps. But that is why we are here. We protect not only a relic, but the sanctity of the knowledge it holds. Our work ensures that it will never fall into hands unworthy of its power."

Rafael, ever the optimist, managed a faint smile despite his wounds. "We are the silent defenders of something far greater than ourselves. And while that burden is heavy, it's also... an honor."

Emmanuel nodded, a glint of pride in his eyes. "When we took our oaths, we knew the weight of what we would carry. But the Codex's value is beyond the grasp of ordinary men and power-hungry leaders. It represents the highest aspirations of faith—a beacon of truth that, in the wrong hands, could lead to ruin."

Marco, leaning heavily against the wall but listening intently, let out a sigh. "So what do we do now? Fortify the monastery? Disappear into the shadows until the next threat arises?"

Santiago considered this, then answered, "We will remain vigilant, as we always have. But we won't be waiting idly. We'll spread word, discreetly, of the Viper's failure—of how his forces vanished into the night without a trace." He gave a wry smile. "Fear and rumor can be as powerful as any weapon. Let them know the Codex is protected by shadows they can't conquer."

Isabela nodded, understanding the strategy. "If they fear what lies in the darkness, they may think twice before challenging it."

Their conversation shifted to practicalities as they discussed fortifying the monastery's defenses and reinforcing their position without drawing unwanted attention. Each suggestion carried an underlying urgency, a recognition that while they had won today, tomorrow could bring a new wave of threats.

As the discussion wound down, the Guard took a rare moment for themselves, sharing a quiet camaraderie that only those who had fought side by side could understand. The battle had deepened their bonds, forging a unity that would not waver in the face of any adversary.

Santiago, seeing the exhaustion in their faces, suggested they take turns resting while keeping watch. "We've earned a moment's peace," he said, a slight smile breaking his usual stoic demeanor. "Let's use it."

One by one, they settled into positions of rest, some closing their eyes for a brief respite while others maintained a vigilant watch. The Codex lay in its hidden chamber, untouched and safe, yet they all felt its presence—a silent reminder of their purpose, their duty.

In the stillness of the monastery, Santiago allowed himself a moment to reflect. He knew the burden of leadership, the weight of responsibility that came with guiding others in the face of overwhelming odds. But he also felt an immense pride in each member of the Guard—their unwavering dedication, their resilience, their unbreakable faith.

After some time, Santiago glanced at his team, his gaze softening. "We've faced a great enemy today, but the true strength of our Guard is not in any one battle. It's in our dedication to something greater than ourselves, a purpose that cannot be swayed by ambition or corrupted by power."

Emmanuel, listening quietly, nodded. "The world will always have those who seek power without understanding its cost. And that is why the Codex must remain hidden."

Santiago met Emmanuel's eyes, understanding the shared responsibility that bound them all. "Then we must move it to a place no one would expect it."

As the night wore on, they fell into a reflective silence, each of them absorbing the lessons of the day, the weight of the Codex's protection. The Guard would remain vigilant, steadfast in their purpose, ready to rise to any challenge that might come.

And so, in the quiet sanctuary of the monastery, they rested, knowing that tomorrow they would have to find a new place to hide the Codex. The Codex's true power would remain a secret, a light hidden in the shadows.

The Guard, weary but unbroken, had weathered the storm. Their resolve was their shield, their faith their anchor, and together, they stood prepared for whatever lay ahead. The Codex was safe, for now—but they knew that, as always, their mission was never truly over.

The cobblestone streets of Rome glistened faintly under a light drizzle as the Guard entered the city at dawn, their cloaks pulled tight against the chill. They moved as they always did: silently, unobtrusively, avoiding prying eyes. The mission was complete, their burden fulfilled. The Codex was no longer their concern. For centuries, the Iberian Guard had served one purpose: the protection of the Church. And in their minds, the Codex—while extraordinary—was but one of many dangers that threatened its sanctity.

Santiago, as ever, led the way through the Vatican gates, his expression calm but thoughtful. Beside him, Emmanuel walked with his usual quiet resolve, while Rafael and Isabela, still nursing their wounds, kept pace without complaint. They felt the weight of their accomplishment but also a sense of finality. The Codex was hidden, its dangerous knowledge placed beyond the reach of even the most zealous reformist.

The Guard was ushered into Pope Leo X's private chambers by a solemn aide. The room was modest, its grandeur muted compared to the splendor of the Vatican. Pope Leo rose from his chair as they entered, his sharp gaze scanning each of them as though searching for answers before they were spoken.

"Captain Santiago," the Pope said, his tone steady, "I trust you bring news of success?"

Santiago inclined his head deeply. "Your Holiness, the Codex is secure. It is now hidden in a location where it will pose no threat to the Church or the faithful."

The Pope stepped forward, his expression softening with visible relief. "You have done the Church a great service. I feared the reformists' hunger for disruption would surpass even your skill, but it seems I underestimated your resolve."

Santiago's voice was calm, even. "The Viper and his forces underestimated us as well, Your Holiness. Their zeal drove them into ruin. The Codex, however, was not something we could risk leaving in their path. Its dangers extend beyond even their ambitions."

The Pope's brow furrowed, his curiosity evident. "This location... you are certain it cannot be found? Not by our enemies, nor by those who might seek it for misguided reasons?"

Santiago straightened, his eyes meeting the Pope's. "It is hidden in plain sight, Your Holiness. Its value obscured by its ordinary surroundings. None who search for it with greed or ambition will recognize its importance. The Codex is a secret even to itself."

There was a pause, the weight of Santiago's words hanging in the air. Pope Leo's expression tightened, his hands clasping behind his back as he paced the room slowly. "And yet, Captain, such knowledge as the Codex contains is a temptation to all, even to those who mean no harm. Surely, the Church must know where it lies, if only to ensure its security?"

Santiago's eyes did not waver, his tone respectful but unyielding. "Your Holiness, with the deepest respect, no one is immune to temptation. The Codex's power is not in its physical form but in the knowledge it contains. Knowledge that could destabilize the very foundations of the Church if misunderstood or misused. Its location must remain unknown to protect the sanctity of the Church, even from within."

The Pope stopped pacing, turning to face Santiago. His expression was unreadable, though a flicker of frustration passed across his features. "Even I am not to know its location?"

Santiago inclined his head, his voice quiet but resolute. "Not even you, Your Holiness. The Codex is not our mission; the Church is. To safeguard its integrity, the Codex must vanish, even from the minds of those who wish to protect it. This burden, we have carried—and it ends here."

A silence settled in the chamber, the weight of Santiago's refusal hanging heavily. Pope Leo's gaze lingered on the Captain, searching for weakness, for hesitation. He found none.

After a long pause, the Pope exhaled softly and returned to his seat. "Your wisdom has always served the Church well, Captain. Perhaps it serves us now. If the Codex is truly beyond reach, then so be it. Let it become a myth, a tale to deter those who would challenge the Church's authority."

Emmanuel, who had been standing silently, stepped forward, his voice measured. "Your Holiness, the Guard exists not to protect relics, but to ensure the Church endures. The Codex, while powerful, is but one of many threats we have faced. Its secrecy is paramount, but it is no longer our duty to safeguard it. Our focus must return to the Church and its people."

Pope Leo studied Emmanuel for a moment, then nodded slowly. "Your perspective is sound, Emmanuel. The Codex's time has passed. The Church, however, must stand eternal."

Isabela, leaning lightly against a pillar for support, spoke next, her voice firm despite her injuries. "Your Holiness, we acted to prevent knowledge from falling into the wrong hands. The Codex is hidden, but we are not its keepers. Our loyalty lies with the Church, not with the relic."

Rafael, his arm still in a sling, added, "The reformists will hunt for it, but they will find nothing. Let their efforts exhaust them, chasing shadows while the Church remains strong."

The Pope leaned back in his chair, his expression contemplative. "Your words ring true. The Guard's mission is not to be the shepherd of lost relics, but the shield of the Church. And yet, I cannot ignore the weight of what you have done. The Codex represents the kind of danger that can never truly be forgotten."

Santiago bowed his head slightly. "That is why it must remain beyond reach, Your Holiness. And why we must never speak of it again."

The Pope's lips pressed into a thin line, but he nodded. "Very well. The Codex is no longer a concern. The Church is grateful for your service, as always. Rest now, and prepare yourselves for what may come next. The reformists are relentless, and their efforts to weaken the Church will not cease."

The Guard bowed deeply before taking their leave. As they exited the chamber, the tension among them eased, though their expressions remained grave.

In the Vatican's marble corridor, Emmanuel broke the silence. "Do you think he truly accepted it, Santiago? That the Codex is beyond even his grasp?"

Santiago's gaze was distant, his voice calm. "He has no choice but to accept it. The temptation of such knowledge would test even the holiest among us. But the Church's survival depends on its absence. He knows this, even if he struggles to admit it."

Isabela glanced back toward the chamber doors. "And what of us? The Codex may be hidden, but its legacy remains. What if someone uncovers it?"

Santiago paused, looking at each of them in turn. "Then it will no longer be our concern. We have fulfilled our duty. The Church must endure, not because of relics, but because of faith. Let the Codex become a tale, a legend that fades into obscurity. And if it resurfaces... it will face another age, another generation, and another Guard."

Rafael grinned faintly, despite the pain in his shoulder. "Until then, we'll do what we've always done: protect the Church from those who would see it fall."

The Guard continued down the corridor, their footsteps echoing faintly in the stillness. Their mission was complete, but their purpose endured. The Codex, now hidden and forgotten, was no longer their burden. Their loyalty, as always, belonged to the Church, to its people, and to the faith that bound them together. And as they walked toward their next challenge, they carried with them the quiet certainty of those who had faced the impossible and prevailed.

## *The End*

Made in the USA
Columbia, SC
01 December 2024